NEXT SUMMER
A SUMMER BOYS NOVEL

HAILEY ABBOTT

SCHOLASTIC INC.

New York Toronto London Auckland Sydney
Mexico City New Delhi Hong Kong Buenos Aires

No part of this publication may be reproduced, or stored in a retrieval system, or
transmitted in any form or by any means, electronic, mechanical, photocopying,
recording, or otherwise, without written permission of the publisher.
For information regarding permission, write to Scholastic Inc., Attention:
Permissions Department, 557 Broadway, New York, NY 10012.

ISBN 0-439-75540-9

ALLOYENTERTAINMENT

Produced by Alloy Entertainment
151 West 26th Street
New York, NY 10001

SCHOLASTIC and associated logos are trademarks and/or registered
trademarks of Scholastic, Inc.

Text design by Steve Scott.
The text type was set in Bulmer.

12 11 10 9 8 7 6 5 4 3   6 7 8 9 10/ 0

Printed in the U.S.A.
First printing, June 2005

1

It only took one kiss for the hammock to start rocking — a little more violently than Beth Tuttle liked, making the moment feel more *roller coaster* than *romantic*.

"I think the original hammock experience beat this one," her boyfriend George said, slowly ending the kiss as he and Beth swung back and forth underneath the shade of the trees in Beth's backyard. For the millionth time, Beth admired George's eyes — brown and deep, and best of all, always laughing.

"You mean last summer?" Beth asked, planting a soft kiss on his nose. "Yeah, I guess our hammock in Pebble Beach is a little more comfortable for hook ups."

Beth grinned as she untangled herself from George and swung her long legs out of the hammock. She stood up and stretched in the warm June sunshine. Scraping her blonde hair back from her face, she squinted across the yard to the garage where her parents had begun piling up boxes in preparation for another summer in Maine. Beth couldn't believe they were leaving for Pebble Beach in the morning. A whole year had passed since she and George had finally figured out they were meant for each other while cuddling in that *other* hammock. Beth sighed at the magical memory. If only George would be coming back to Pebble Beach *this* summer.

"Come on," George said, climbing to his feet. "Let's go inside."

He looked down at her with that sly, sexy smile of his and slowly ran his hand down her arm. He took her hand and brought it up to his lips, his mouth gently grazing her skin. Beth felt her breath catch. That was all the encouragement she needed to follow George to Antarctica, the moon, or wherever he wanted to go.

They entered the kitchen, dodging all the summer provisions that were scattered around the room — a huge picnic basket and bags of groceries were strewn about the floor; Beth's father's boat shoes were lying on top of a mountain of sealed cardboard boxes; and a collection of battered tennis rackets cluttered up the countertop. Her mother had obviously been very busy, and Beth knew she needed to start bringing down her clothes and beach gear. But, right then, she had other, more important, things on her mind than packing.

"So you think painting is going to be more fun than the beach?" she asked George sourly, picking up one of the rackets. She ran her hand across the tight web of strings and pressed it against the pads of her fingers. There was a part of her that wanted to beat George over the head with the racket — how could he possibly give up a summer with her to work a job that required him to breath in toxic fumes?

Beth knew that George knew her well enough to recognize her urge to smack some sense into him, which was probably why he took the makeshift weapon out of her grasp, reached over, and held her face between his hands. He kissed her softly, and then tilted his head away to hold her gaze. George always knew exactly how to distract her.

"This summer is about money, not fun," he said with a sad smile, his curly hair flopping forward. "All the cash I'm going to make will lead to the ultimate Year of George in the fall. I can practically guarantee it." Beth reached over and pushed his hair back so that she could get a better view of him. After tomorrow, she'd be without her boyfriend for almost three solid months.

"I thought it was supposed to be the summer of George and Beth," she said, grinning up at him. "Now it's the *fall* of *George?*"

"C'mon, you know the seasons of George revolve around you, Bethy," George replied with a smirk. "Why do you think I signed up for this gig? I'd like, I don't know, to get you something nice for a change."

"You mean something that doesn't come from the Dollar Tree?" Beth teased.

"Hey, a lot of good stuff comes from the Tree. Like that dashboard hula girl and the lemon-scented Jesus car freshener," George replied defensively.

"Well, they'd be a lot more practical if I had a car." Beth grinned, remembering her birthday presents.

"I've been trying to send your parents some hints. See how crafty I am?"

"If by crafty, you mean stupid," Beth quipped.

"Ouch. I thought you loved the G-man," George said as he clutched at his heart and made a sad face.

"What do you know about painting, anyway?" Beth whined, changing the subject. She hated the way she sounded — needy. She couldn't help it. "You barely got through art class." Not that slapping paint on dorms for the brainiacs at MIT was exactly art, Beth thought. But that was beside the point.

"I know it pays way more money than slaving away at the Mini Mart," George replied. His sly smile was back. He took Beth's hands in his and began backing up, leading her out of the kitchen. "I've worked at that place so long I'm like fifty seconds away from becoming that guy in *Clerks.*"

He drew Beth toward the stairs. As Beth followed him, she studied the back of his pale blue Old Navy T-shirt. Beth smiled when she thought about the hundreds of times she had taken that shirt off George over the course of the past twelve months. That blue shirt had landed on the floor of Beth's room after soccer practice, before going to the movies, during their study sessions for history, and every other occasion in between. And, more often than not, George's pants came off, too, Beth reflected, gazing appreciatively at his butt, lost somewhere beneath his baggy dark jeans. Beth loved nothing more than fooling around with George, for hours on end. They had — as her cousin Ella might put it —"done everything but."

Somehow, even after a year of dating, sex hadn't happened yet.

Beth was pretty positive that she was ready. In fact, she and George had come seriously close too many times to count. But there was always either some sort of absurd interruption — like her dad knocking on the door at a totally wrong moment — or some kind of crazy obstacle. Both she and George became obsessed with The Moment, as they liked to call it. That one perfect moment, when the mood would feel just right, and they would both just *know*.

So far, The Moment hadn't happened.

When they reached her bedroom, George immediately shut the door and wrapped Beth in his arms. They fell across her bed together. Beth curled herself around his body as he kissed his way up from her shoulders to her mouth. When their lips met, Beth heard herself moan just a little bit. She loved the taste of him (red licorice — George was obsessed with Twizzlers) and the feel of his body against hers (like a warm flannel blanket in the middle of winter — no matter what the season). Beth rolled over so she was on top of him. George ran his fingers through her hair and then brought his mouth to hers for another succulent, sweet kiss.

In minutes, they were in full make-out mode, and Beth was relishing the feel of George's hands traveling down the length of her body. *Why not now?* Beth wondered suddenly. They'd put off having sex for so long. Too long, maybe. *Why not give us something to remember, since we'll be apart all summer?*

Beth rotated her hips against George's. George loved this maneuver so much that he had given it a name: The Gyration Sensation. She wiggled a little bit more and heard George groan.

"Shhhhh. My mom is in the basement, not in a sound-proof booth."

"I'm sorry. You know what that move does to me," George sighed, rolling Beth over so she was on her back. She felt dizzy and her body tingled wherever he touched her. But now that she had brought up her mom, she couldn't help feeling all too aware of her parents' presence in the house. Which was so the opposite of sexy.

And did she really want to sleep with George *now*? Who wanted to lose her virginity and *then* be alone all summer? The thought suddenly depressed Beth. One time with George would not be enough. If they had sex now, she'd want to keep doing it with him all summer long.

So Beth slowed down the action by shifting to her side and curling into a fetal position. This was a move that happened more often than The Gyration Sensation, so it should also have had a name, but Beth was glad that George was too sweet to ever tease her about it. His usual response was to cuddle up right behind her. And he did just that. George sighed against her ear as his arms hugged her waist.

"Good call, Bethy," he said, nuzzling her neck. "I have to say, the fact that your mom is doing laundry downstairs isn't much of a turn-on."

Beth let out a hefty exhale. George *was* the world's best boyfriend. He'd never think to pressure her about sex.

"This summer is going to suck," Beth whispered.

Without having to see his face, Beth knew that George was wearing a guilty expression. It was the same one he'd been wearing ever since he'd told her about his summer plans.

"Well, it will," Beth persisted. "I was bummed when I found out Jamie wasn't coming to Maine, because of the Amherst writing program. But your not being there is plenty worse."

"Ella and Kelsi will be there," George said. "And the rest of your entire family. . . ."

"It's not the same," Beth cut in. She hated it when he was reasonable. "It's supposed to be *all* the cousins. Jamie, Ella, Kelsi, and me. The four Tuttle girls. It's a tradition, and Jamie's breaking it. And you're like an honorary Tuttle cousin, so you're breaking tradition, too." She pouted.

"Okay, please don't refer to me as your cousin again, because that's just creepy and gross," George chuckled. "As for breaking tradition, I'm just trying to start a new one. You know, where I get to spend money on us without having to ask my parents to dip into my college fund."

"Don't you get it? I don't care about any of that," Beth said. "I just want to be with you."

George repositioned himself so that he was lying down in front of Beth and looking directly into her eyes.

"God, I'm going to miss you," Beth said.

He leaned in and kissed her again. His lips were warm and

so right, so *George*. Beth didn't want to be without him, even if it was just for the summer. Because, for her, being without George was the same as forgetting how to laugh. It was that unimaginable.

But Beth also couldn't believe how clingy she was being. When had this happened? When did she morph from an independent, smart-mouthed jock into this girl who couldn't operate unless she was connected to George at the hip? Was she scared? Did she have, in the back of her mind, the slightest of doubts? George might have seemed cool about their not having sex yet. But maybe if George had a few months away from her, he'd have hours upon hours to think about what their relationship was missing.

Before Beth could get lost in that trail of worries, George calmed her by pulling her across his chest and planting small kisses from her temple and across her cheek to her mouth.

"I'm going to miss you, too," he murmured. "Which is why I promise I'll make it up there, even if it's only for a day."

"When?" Beth said, threading her arms around his neck.

"As soon as humanly possible," he replied. "Really. I know I put on a good act, but I'm a mess without you, Bethy."

Beth grinned, and then ran her hands through George's curly hair, making it frizz out. "You're a mess, period."

"Oh, so that's how you want to be, huh?" George asked mischievously, suddenly kneeling on the bed. He posed as if he were about to attempt a complicated wrestling move.

Beth tensed up but couldn't help giggling. "Take it easy,

George. You don't want me to break your painting hand now, do you?"

"The threats only fuel the fire!" George boomed. Then he dove in for a tickle of massive proportions.

Beth squirmed around and shrieked like a little girl as George's fingers worked the backs of her knees and her ribs. "Stop! Stop!" she cried. But she really didn't want him to stop. She wanted to soak up all of George's energy and put it in a bottle so that she could ration it out over the next few months. Even though the room was filled with their laughter, Beth knew that once she set foot on Pebble Beach without George by her side, she would have to remind herself how to smile.

2

Ella eyed her reflection in the passenger side mirror one more time, frowned, and then folded the mirror back up.

"I'm serious," she told her sister. "I think my pores are getting bigger, like, as we drive."

"Because that's scientifically possible," Kelsi said mockingly, keeping her eyes on the road. "Your pores are exactly the same size as they were when we left, El. I promise."

Ella rolled her eyes and slumped back into her seat. Like Kelsi knew anything about pores.

It was high time for them to hurry up and get to Pebble Beach, already. The Tuttle sisters had left New Canaan, Connecticut, at the butt-crack of dawn, and Ella had the puffy bags under her eyes to prove it. She'd gone to bed at her usual late hour, and was so not a morning person. So far, the ride had been nothing but boring highway, mile after mile. At least they were on the Maine state road now, the one that wandered in and out of the beach towns along the coast and ended up in Pebble Beach. The scenery had vastly improved. There were hills and trees and creeks — much, much prettier than rest stops.

Ella couldn't wait for summer to start, which, in her opinion, would not officially occur until she placed her feet in the grass outside her family's cottage. Their dad was already up there, so all she and Kelsi had to do was unpack their clothes and settle back in.

"You drive like a little old lady," she said to Kelsi, just to be obnoxious.

Kelsi shook her head, and turned up the volume on the CD player, deafening Ella's ears with Dar Williams.

Ella regarded her sister for a moment. The Kelsi singing along to some estrogen anthem barely resembled the sobbing mess of a girl who, last summer, had discovered that her extremely hot boyfriend had cheated on her. Kelsi seemed tougher. Braver. In fact, Ella noticed that these days, Kelsi looked like the sort of girl who might go homicidal if she had any idea that the girl Peter had cheated on her with had been . . . her own sister.

Which is why Ella prayed every night to any supreme being who would listen that Kelsi would never, ever find out.

Ella shook her head and tried to think about something else, but for some reason, she couldn't stop dwelling on her new and improved big sis. As soon as they'd returned to New Canaan at the end of last summer, Kelsi had shocked everyone by dying her natural blonde hair to a dark glossy brown à la

Ashlee Simpson, a decision she'd made without consulting Ella. Ella didn't think Kelsi was qualified to make drastic leaps in fashion, mainly because Kelsi had spent her entire life as Ms. Crunchy: She never wore makeup, doused herself in patchouli oil, and complied with all the other ugly rules of hippiedom. Ella had always figured Kelsi just liked to be ignored. Why else would she deliberately make herself look so plain — just so she could be one with the environment or whatever?

But now, things were different. It wasn't like Kelsi had tossed her patchouli oil into the trash — despite Ella's best efforts — but Kelsi's vibe had changed quite a bit. Instead of constantly chiding Ella about recycling, she was now more up for a laugh or some celebrity gossip. Today, she was wearing cutoffs and one of those cute vintage baby tees with MORE TREES, LESS BUSH written on the front. She was the superconfident, "I'm not going to take your shit anymore" Kelsi, and Ella was still getting used to her.

Ella shifted her attention to the road again, and sat up straight when she realized they were *finally* entering town. Pebble Beach.

"We're here!" she cried, and gave a little whoop of joy.

Then she grinned at Kelsi, and they both rolled down their windows to let sunshine and the smell of the ocean rush inside and fill the car.

Ella leaned out the window as Kelsi weaved through the slow pace of traffic. Ella noticed a few new shops along the main thoroughfare, but, far more important, new guys.

Brand-new summer boys in all their tanned and shirtless glory. They were practically lined up and down the street for her to gawk at, she thought. Like Pebble Beach was one big eye-candy store.

"Drool much?" Kelsi teased, apparently noticing Ella's appreciation of the long-limbed blond guy who ambled in front of the car at a stop sign.

"I never drool," Ella replied, smiling. "I just . . . admire."

And admire she did. There were boys everywhere, jostling one another on the sidewalks and slouching off toward the beach. Ella wanted to eat every last one of them up.

"Really?" Kelsi sounded amused. "Didn't you make some sort of vow when we got into the car this morning? Something about you swearing off guys this summer?"

Ella winced at the mere mention of that. Why did Kelsi have to be so damn attentive?

"Oh, right," she said. "Of course I'm sticking to that vow. But, hello, I'm not *blind.*"

As Kelsi laughed, Ella reminded herself that this summer, she was on a high self-esteem, low hook-up diet. She wasn't going to indulge in messing around with random members of the male species, no matter how seemingly delicious. She was the new, improved Ella, who was only going to commit to *one* guy. One relationship. Love and trust and blah blah blah. There would be no more of Ella's patented flirting or her treating boys like the one-use towels you get at the public pool.

"Well, El, since you're on sabbatical, that leaves a whole lot more guys for the rest of us," Kelsi said with another laugh as she turned from the main road onto the little dirt track that led to the cottages.

Ella felt a little chill race through her as the car bumped along the dirt, but she shook it off. So what if Kelsi wanted to mix it up with some hottie? That was what summer was for. And Kelsi deserved to relax, have fun, and rake in the admirers. She'd gotten her heart broken last summer, after all.

And so had Ella, but the difference was Ella's heart wound was self-inflicted. She'd pretty much known Peter was a creep, and she'd still gone after him.

Ella had discovered that when you do something hideous and no one else knows about it, you had only yourself for comfort. It was a lonely way to live. Then again, Ella had herself to blame for being in that position, and there wasn't any use dwelling on it now, especially when an entire new summer was ahead of her.

Kelsi pulled up in front of the cottage their family rented every summer, and they both climbed out of the car. Ella treated herself to a nice long stretch, and gazed around at the familiar sights. The tall pine trees ringed the lawn, with the cottages nestled into place at their roots. The beach was just beyond the dunes. The Maine sun was at its best up above, showering everything with light and warmth.

Last summer was in the past, Ella kept telling herself. Over. She was a different person now — a better one, and a better sister, too.

"This is going to be the best summer yet. I can feel it,"

14

Kelsi said, coming around the car and grinning at Ella. She slung an arm around Ella's shoulders and squeezed her. "Aren't you excited?"

"I can't wait," Ella said with her best smile, and in that moment, she decided to be just as excited as she sounded.

3

"We're leaving without you!"

Ella's voice floated over from the yard on the evening air. Kelsi was in her room; she knew her sister and Beth were waiting for her to finish dressing for the first party of the summer. She had already discarded just about every top she'd brought with her, and was halfway through a repeat cycle.

The thing was, she felt strange. The not-being-comfortable-in-your-own-skin kind of strange. Every minute that went by, Kelsi became a little bit more anxious and nervous. She had no idea *what* was making her feel like her legs were made out of lo mein noodles, but whatever *it* was, she just wanted it to take a hike so that she could enjoy the start of another Pebble Beach summer.

After all, Kelsi had everything under control. She had just graduated from high school at the top of her class, and she was headed to Smith in the fall. Kelsi should have been practically drunk on her own shining future. She had felt so *together* at graduation. Like she knew exactly who she was and where she was going.

Funny. Kelsi didn't feel remotely that way at the moment.

"Kels! Come on!" This time it was Beth. Her cousin's voice was less strident than Ella's, but she still sounded impatient. Kelsi snuck a look out the window. The last streaks of the red sunset were fading from the sky, which meant the party down on the pier would just be getting underway.

Kelsi took a deep breath, and looked at her reflection in the mirror one more time.

She was just going to have to go with the deep V-necked black T-shirt and her favorite pair of jeans. Both were from Anthropologie, Kelsi's absolutely most-favorite store in the world. The black push-up bra Ella had talked her into buying at Victoria's Secret was working big-time, and Kelsi had to admit, she liked the result. Her newly re-dyed dark brown hair was pulled back in a sassy, casual ponytail that had taken at least forty minutes to perfect, and she slicked another coat of lip gloss across her lips.

Now, if she could just *feel* the way she *looked* . . .

"What are you doing in here?" Ella demanded, appearing in the door of the bedroom the two of them shared. She leaned against the doorjamb and snapped her gum a few times, a habit that drove Kelsi absolutely crazy. Luckily, at the moment, she was too wound up to get sufficiently agitated.

"I'm ready," Kelsi said, grinning at her baby sister as if she'd never been more at ease. She made for the door, but stopped when she saw Ella glance at the pile of rejected shirts that now covered her bedspread and half of Ella's.

"You had a fashion emergency and you didn't call me?" Ella put a hand over her heart. "I think my feelings are hurt."

"I was having a bad-me day." Kelsi gave a wry grin.

"Puh-leeze, you look fantastic. Better than me, even," Ella said through her trademark snort of a laugh.

Without a moment to lose, Kelsi and Ella dashed out to the yard, where Beth was standing with her arms wrapped around herself, staring up at the sky.

"I always forget how clear it is up here," she said. "The night looks almost . . . messy with all those stars, doesn't it?"

Kelsi tipped her head back, breathing in the clean air and the ever-present scent of the evergreens. Beth was right. Up above the pines, the sky was littered with stars she never got to see in New Canaan. She had a second to remind herself about all the possibilities that were awaiting her, but then it was time to move.

The girls began walking down the dirt road that led from the Tuttles' three rental cottages to Pebble Beach's main strip. The trees towered over the narrow track, and grass clung to the little cliff between the tire ruts and the forest.

"As you can see, Beth dressed for the occasion," Ella told Kelsi, a teasing lilt in her voice.

Kelsi glanced at Beth. Her cousin was wearing track pants and a blue scoop-necked tee. Her long blonde hair — so different from Ella's sexy mane — fell straight down her back.

"What?" Beth asked, opening her arms wide and looking down at herself. "I put on a clean shirt."

Kelsi adored the fact that Beth saw no reason to put on makeup or a cute outfit for parties. Clearly, having a boyfriend hadn't changed Beth that much.

"And if you feel like it, you can just go for a quick jog between beers," Ella said, shooting her cousin a sideways look with her heavily mascaraed eyes.

"My Jimmy Choos don't go with this outfit," Beth told Ella, bouncing up on the toes of her sneakers. "Anyway, I'll leave the fabulousness to you and your tiny dress." She looked back at Kelsi. "And you, with the lip stuff. What's with that?"

"It adds moisture." Kelsi shrugged. Last year, Kelsi's idea of dressing up was adding the occasional bandanna to her ensemble. Lip gloss was never in her repertoire. "I'm still a vegetarian, if that makes you feel better."

"Everything about this summer is weird," Beth grumbled.

"Tell us about your year, Bethy," Ella commanded. "How is *George*? I want juicy boyfriend details. Have you guys done it, or what?"

"Ella!" Beth squealed, but it sounded like she was only pretending to be scandalized. "How is that your business?"

Kelsi trailed slightly behind them while Beth talked. She tilted her head back a little bit to bask in the surrounding night. She loved Pebble Beach. She loved the dirt roads washed with sand, and the stretch of cold sea in the distance. Boats bobbed on their moorings, the clank of lines against the masts announcing their presence in the dark. As she turned left toward town, the bright white lights of the pier danced ahead, beckoning her into another summer.

Kelsi couldn't contain the slight tremor of apprehension that went through her. There would be people everywhere and a band playing onstage — she could hear the thump of the bass even from this far away. It was like déjà vu, but she fervently hoped that the band wouldn't include Peter, her asshole of an ex.

What bothered Kelsi (maybe more than it should) was that she'd never had a *real* boyfriend. Listening to Beth ramble on about her relationship just made it achingly obvious to Kelsi that there was something wrong with her. She had such shitty luck with guys. Kelsi had been so sure Peter was this charming, cool rocker, but he had turned out to be a liar and a cheat. Before Peter, she'd spent three months dating Brian before he'd gone off to college. He'd broken up with her because she hadn't been ready to sleep with him. Two guys — and both of them were losers. *What a track record, indeed.*

The truth of the matter was, Kelsi was eighteen years old, still a virgin, and her younger cousin seemed a lot more adept than her at picking out a really good guy. Not to mention her sister, who got boys as easily as she breathed. Kelsi was starting to think she was destined to spend the rest of her life as a celibate dickhead magnet.

"What's wrong with you now?" Ella's exasperated voice floated back to Kelsi through the dark. "Are you up for this party or not?"

"I'm looking at the stars," Kelsi replied. She looked up

again. The stars crowded the sky, so many lights that it almost made Kelsi dizzy.

Kelsi took another deep breath, and released it back into the crisp night. There was sand on her toes and salt in her hair. A new summer waited just ahead. Now she just had to catch up to it.

The pier, as usual, looked like a scene out of *Laguna Beach*, except the setting was more earthy. Less glamorous. But the boys were rounded up in packs as if they were in line for a casting call. Ella wondered if this tiny little section of New England had suddenly become the spot where the world's most eligible guys could hang out and look unequivocally scrumptious.

Ella led the way into the crowd, feeling self-assured as the party swept her into its loud chaos. She was lapping up the attention she was getting from all the boys who were checking out the little green tube-dress she'd picked out just for the occasion.

Ella might have decided to turn over a new leaf, but that didn't mean she had to *dress* like a saint, did it?

A tall guy with toned arms and wavy auburn hair sidled up to Ella without a word and tried to wrap his arm around her waist, so she shimmied a little bit and laughed at him as she pulled away. His buddy, who was cute-ish, but short, whistled low and deliberately, which made her smile. Beth and Kelsi nudged each other and rolled their eyes, weaving around Ella and the two drooling guys.

"Sorry, boys," Ella said matter-of-factly, but with a grin. "This is strictly a girls' night out." Then she waved the guys away, feeling merry and powerful, surrounded by the music and salty air. She dodged a couple of kids making out and caught up with her sister and cousin, who'd come to a stop near the railing at the edge of the pier.

"I hate that Jamie's not here," Beth said, sadly looking around at the crowd. "She loved the pier."

"She's not dead, she's in a summer program," Kelsi pointed out, poking Beth in the side. "God, could you be any mopier?"

"She misses George," Ella confided, loudly enough to alert half of Pebble Beach. She realized her volume and giggled. "Oops."

Beth blushed, which she hardly ever did, and glanced down, clearly affected by Ella's words.

"He's not coming up at all?" Kelsi asked Beth softly.

Ella tried to listen, but her eyes were scanning the crowd, browsing for hotties. She was beginning to think that what she called her I-can-stop-anytime-I-want-to obsession with guys was actually a full-on addiction. Maybe she needed to wear a medicine patch on her arm or check herself into rehab. What was *wrong* with her? Why couldn't she just stay focused on her cousins? They were just as much fun as boys. More fun, maybe.

Okay, who was she kidding?

"He called me earlier and said that he won't have any time off until August," Beth replied with a shrug, wrinkling up her nose.

"I like George," Ella said, managing to take her mind off the Taye Diggs look-alike who was winking at her. She sternly reminded herself of The Vow. "He's a great guy."

"Wow, that's a first, Ella." Beth shook her head in amazement. Ella usually made fun of George for being so boyish. "You almost sound like you mean it."

"I do, actually. In fact, I think I want one for myself," Ella added.

"He's not a Kate Spade bag. He's a person," Beth pointed out.

Ella felt a bit offended by that remark, though she understood that it had some merit. Yes, she was notorious for being a little shallow and materialistic and boy-crazy. But since her sinful encounter with Peter last year, Ella had been working hard on trying to become less self-obsessed. A part of Ella *was* truly growing tired of the whole game. She wanted to meet someone she could really get close to. The only thing preventing that from happening was the *other* part of her that wanted to kiss whomever she pleased. Still, Ella was trying to reel herself in. She wanted — needed — to change for the better.

"Yeah, but George is the perfect boyfriend. Steady. Reliable.

I mean, every summer, it's all about the hooking up and the chasing and the drama," she complained to Kelsi and Beth.

"Did you even hook up last summer?" Kelsi interrupted.

Ella froze. Like she even wanted to touch that question. She sighed dramatically instead of answering.

"I was pretty preoccupied with the whole Peter mess," Kelsi went on. "I can't remember what your summer drama was, El."

Crap. "I'm totally going to settle down this summer," Ella announced abruptly, hoping to get Kelsi off the subject. "Just like Britney has."

Beth just shook her head, and Kelsi swallowed a laugh.

"I'm serious, you guys. Listen, Beth. If you see me slipping and *accidentally* flirting with some hot summer boy, you have to promise to cut me off. Drag me away if necessary."

"Why is this *my* job?" Beth asked, but she was grinning.

"Hey, if Jamie were here, I'd give *her* the job. She's a lot stricter," Ella replied.

"Well, if I'm going to spend the summer being your chastity belt, then I think you owe me a road trip down to Amherst." Beth looked from one cousin to the other. "If Jamie can't come to Pebble Beach, we should bring Pebble Beach to Jamie. For, like, a weekend or something. What do you say?"

"Awesome. I love road trips!" Ella replied enthusiastically.

"It's a great idea," Kelsi agreed. "Count me in. And I brought my car up, so I can drive."

"Great," Beth said with a grin. "But no way *you're* doing all the driving, Kelsi. By the time we get there, Jamie will have published her novel already."

Ella laughed at her sister's notoriously slow, careful driving, and dug out a cigarette from her bag. She put it to her lips, and was pleased when a guy leaned over and offered her his lighter. Ella did everything she could not to ogle his killer grin and sculpted shoulders, which were hiding beneath a blue hoodie.

"Aren't you sweet," Ella said, batting her eyes and letting out a perfect smoke ring.

"*Ah-choo, cutitout,*" Beth said through a blatantly fake sneeze.

Ella sighed heavily. Jamie would have been a lot more subtle than that.

"Let's find something to drink," Kelsi said, which was definitely a plan Ella could support. "It's time to get this summer started."

Ella gave the lighter-sporting cutie a special little smile, and then followed her sister deeper into the crowd.

Down on the beach, some guys had started a big bonfire closer to the dunes. While Kelsi went to grab beers, Ella settled herself on one of the rocks nearby. Immediately, two new guys came over to talk to her. All Ella had to do was just *be* and guys would practically come wandering out of the shrubbery to look at her adoringly. *Is there a silent whistle I could blow that would make them go away?* Ella wondered. *And if so, would I really want to use it?*

"What's your name?" one boy — the skinnier one — asked.

Neither one was her type (they both looked like Clay Aiken and were small enough to fit into her clothes), but Ella wasn't one to let something so minor get in the way of a little innocent flirting. She started to reply when Beth appeared at her side.

"So, what about that pledge?" Beth asked, pinching Ella's arm.

"What can I do?" Ella whispered. "They're everywhere. I can only cope with so much temptation." She waved her arm over the summer people milling around on the sand.

The bonfire crackled and smoked, and just outside the ring of heat, the night air was chilly and inky black. The waves rolled onto the beach, the water dark and mysterious as the tide came in. A pair of girls were playing what looked like drunken tag just a few steps away from the fire, while a group of boys who looked like they got lost on their way to a Phish concert cheered them on. There were even a few couples getting busy back where the rocks littered the beach.

Most important, there were a whole lot of guys. Guys Ella didn't know. And among them, maybe, the one Ella was looking for.

"I don't think you're really *trying* to resist, El," Beth said suspiciously.

As if to prove Beth wrong, Ella immediately rebuffed the two Clay Aiken boys — something she managed to do so smoothly the two of them looked as pleased, as if they'd actually gotten somewhere with her.

"See?" Ella flashed her cousin a grin. "I totally resisted those two."

"That shouldn't have been so hard," Kelsi said from behind them. "I think the red-haired one was about twelve."

"Whatever," Ella said, helping herself to one of the bottles of beer Kelsi was cradling against her chest. The three girls smiled at one another as Beth took a beer for herself.

"To new boys, fun parties, and the perfect tan," Ella said grandly, holding her beer aloft.

"To a good summer," Kelsi said, doing the same.

Beth, whose smile seemed a little dimmer, reluctantly opened her mouth to throw a toast in there, but Ella cut her off with a long, low whistle when she spotted a figure near the shore.

"What is *that* delicious thing?" she asked, her eyes widening. She clutched her beer and sat forward on the rock.

He had huge brown eyes and an artful mess of dark curly hair. He walked through the crowd with a different kind of grace than the other boys around him. He wore a forest green sweater and low-slung jeans, neither of which Ella could label-ID from a distance. But she noticed other details, like how his bare feet sank into the sand when he moved. He looked like some kind of cat, all lean and hungry, and he was headed straight for Ella.

Ella knew one thing for sure: Screw the stupid vow. She would not, and could not, say no to this guy.

"Of course, you're going to resist him, right?" Kelsi snickered as Mr. Dark-and-Mysterious moved through the crowd. "Like you swore you would?"

A naughty smile was creeping across Ella's mouth as the dark-haired boy drew closer.

"If this isn't love, I don't want to know what it is. . . ." she replied.

"He hasn't even said hello yet." Beth shook her head.

"Sometimes words are unnecessary," Ella murmured, and then she just smiled, because the hot guy was now front and center and looking mighty fine. When Ella looked up at him, she felt a shiver run through her.

"Come," the boy said in a thick foreign accent that transformed him from plain old hot into scorching in one second flat. "We . . . talk."

"Why can't we *talk* here?" Ella asked, cocking her head to the side.

He smiled slowly. Ella felt herself quivering. This guy was sex personified.

"The things I wish to talk about are better in private," he explained softly.

That was all the convincing Ella needed.

"Later," she mouthed to Beth and Kelsi over her shoulder. Then she put her hand into his, and let him pull her to her feet.

The stranger escorted Ella just outside the light of the fire. They stood there, looking at each other. Ella watched the fire dance across his face, illuminating his incredible cheekbones and dark eyes. Still holding his hand, she angled herself toward him.

"I saw you and I knew," he said simply.

"I knew it, too," Ella replied, smiling up at him.

What she'd said to Beth had been accurate. Sometimes words — or actual conversations — *weren't* necessary.

As if the boy had read her mind, he slid his arm around Ella's back, then drew her close to kiss her. The kiss was hot and long, and Ella felt her body exult in it. She pulled him closer and kissed him harder, feeling their tongues touch and the heat of the moment swell through her.

I'll be a better girl tomorrow, Ella thought as she grabbed the beautiful stranger by the sleeve of his sweater and pulled him into the dark beyond the fire.

By the time Kelsi made it back across the sand to grab another beer, there was a crowd about five people deep around the cooler, all jostling for access.

This was the worst part about beach bonfires. On TV, they always looked like so much fun — bikini-clad girls lounging around, sipping drinks and chatting. The reality, at least in Pebble Beach, was that it was too chilly to wear a bikini at night, and the competing boom boxes made conversation nearly impossible. Indie rock to the right, hip-hop to the left. *Something for everyone,* Kelsi thought.

It was hard to walk across cold sand in the dark, with her feet slipping and her flip-flops almost sliding off. It was even harder to figure out where the beer was. Finally, she was able to duck through an unexpected opening in a wall of guys. Kelsi grabbed three beers when she got to the nearest cooler, pulling them out of the ice so fast that the ice water sluiced down her jeans, sending a chill right through to her thighs. Then she had to shove her way back out of the mob. When she finally got free, she frowned down at the huge, damp marks on the front of her jeans.

"I hate it when that happens," a deep voice said to her left, giving a small laugh.

Kelsi looked up, and had to take a quick breath to steady herself.

"Hi," he said, flashing a grin. "I'm Tim."

Tim was gorgeous.

As in Heath Ledger–type of gorgeous.

His dirty-blond hair curled at the edges, and his smile was practically divine. His arms looked muscled, but still lean, beneath the long-sleeved T-shirt he wore. His hazel eyes gleamed with laughter and that lazy confidence guys have when they know exactly how hot they are. His expression alone made Kelsi's blood boil with both annoyance and apprehension. She had seen the likes of this cocky attitude before and it had given her nothing but trouble. She narrowed her eyes at him.

"I feel it's my duty to tell you that those beers are pretty much skunked beyond all recognition," Tim said, seemingly unfazed by Kelsi's scrutiny. "Hand to God. But if you step over this way, my buddies can hook you up with something you can actually drink."

"And to what do I owe this honor?" Kelsi asked tartly.

Tim's grin widened. "I can't sleep at night if I let cute girls drink skunked beer."

"What a guy," she replied in a sarcastic tone. Tim didn't seem to notice.

"You bet," he agreed, nudging Kelsi in the right direction with his arm. She liked the feel of his skin against her own, but was instantly annoyed at herself for even noticing. This guy was obviously a jerk. Clearly one of those jock types. She tried to keep her distance by hanging back as he went over to the big cooler where a group of guys were hanging out. Tim extracted a selection of cans from within.

"Hey, Miller!" one of his buddies complained. "Stop giving all our beer away!"

Tim ignored him and smiled at Kelsi.

"Allow me to take those off your hands," he said, indicating the spoiled beers she held. "I'll even get rid of them for you, because I'm full-service like that." He frowned. "Sorry. I wish I knew why skunked beer happens."

"Light," Kelsi replied absently. She felt a little bit dizzy looking at his face, which was ruddy in the glow of the fire. Or maybe she was dizzy because she couldn't believe she was this susceptible to Tim's hot-itude. Regardless, it took her a moment to notice he was staring at her.

"What?" she asked, feeling defensive.

"You said 'light,'" Tim reminded her. His mouth twitched, like he wanted to laugh.

"Um, there's this chemical reaction when bright light hits

beer," Kelsi said, leaning over and thrusting the cans in question into the sand. "That's what makes it smell."

Tim gazed at her for a long moment that stopped just short of uncomfortable.

"How do you know that?" he asked.

Because I am Queen of the Dorks, Kelsi thought.

"I like science," she muttered. Her face felt too hot, and she hoped it just looked like a by-product of the bonfire.

"You're like an encyclopedia," Tim told her with an approving smile. "Walking around in the body of Mandy Moore. This is obviously my lucky night."

Kelsi gritted her teeth. She hated the fact he was flirting with her. And that she wanted to respond. It didn't take much imagination to see where flirting with Tim would lead: Peter, part two. Kelsi refused to make that mistake twice. She didn't want to meet his gaze, so she focused on his gray T-shirt instead.

"U Mass?" she asked, reading the red logo. *Probably going to play football there,* she thought.

He tilted his chin down as if he were trying to read it along with her. "I'm headed there in the fall," Tim said proudly. "Like my brothers before me. Millers go to U Mass, pledge the same frat, and play mediocre football."

Kelsi ignored her twinge of disappointment. She'd pegged this guy from the moment she'd laid eyes on him. Why was it a surprise that she was right? He was way too good-looking to be anything but a shallow jock.

"Thanks for the beer," she said curtly, and took the ones he'd been holding.

"Anytime," he replied immediately, with that same sparkle in his eyes.

Kelsi felt a slight pang — why couldn't the gorgeous ones ever have some substance to them? And more to the point, why wasn't she ever interested in guys with substance? Computer geeks, for example, or poets. Political activists. Why was it always the flashy ones who got her pulse racing? Rockers. Football players. Well, her pulse could race all it wanted, she decided firmly. She wasn't following it anymore.

"See you around," she said abruptly to Jock Boy, and turned away. *Good-bye, Peter part two.*

"Wait, you never even told me your name!" he shouted over the music.

His hazel eyes were bright when she looked at him over her shoulder. He made her heart ache a little bit and, oh yes, he knew it. But Kelsi decided she was stronger than Ella when it came to resisting boys.

"It's Kelsi," she told him. "But don't worry, I don't think you'll need to remember it."

She didn't bother looking back again.

From: jtuttle@amherst.edu
To: bethtuttle34@aol.com
Subject: Summertime Love

Dear Beth,

Happy summer, girl. I'm having a great time here at Amherst. The campus is so green and gorgeous. And there's a really cute town with vintage clothing shops and cafés. Everyone in the program is super-nice and really into writing. And the instructor is all kinds of hot. The way he talks about poetry makes my heart pound. It makes it hard to concentrate on my writing, but I'm managing . . . I think! I've been in and out of touch with that guy Scott from last summer, too, but it's nothing serious with us.

    I'm so jealous that everyone's together in Pebble

Beach! I miss Uncle Carr and Aunt Claire, and the little cousins. And most of all, you, El, and Kels. I want to hear every last detail about what's going on up there with you guys. Seriously: every boy who notices Kelsi (not that she'd notice them back, of course), every summer boy Ella toys with, and how you're surviving without George. Nothing is too insignificant to keep from me. I want to feel like I'm up there — it'll keep me from feeling Maine-sick. Write soon.
Love, Jamie

Beth smiled at the computer screen and took a sip of coffee, missing her smart, bubbly cousin. Then she shrieked when she caught sight of someone lurking in her peripheral vision.

"Um, could you please avoid screaming?" Ella asked, shuffling into the room and collapsing on the sofa, clutching her head all the while.

"You scared me!" Beth collapsed back against the computer chair, and swiveled it around so she could look at her bedraggled cousin.

"Bethy, please. My poor head . . ." Ella held her head in her hands as if it were the size of a pumpkin and much more fragile. Beth suddenly noticed that Ella was still wearing her green tube-dress from the night before, only now she was barefoot and her hair was significantly less sleek. Beth's jaw dropped.

"You slut!" Beth accused in a delighted whisper, on the

off-chance there were adults around somewhere. "You're totally doing the Walk of Shame!"

Ella moaned, and didn't raise her head.

"I saw you getting it on with that Benjamin Bratt clone before you guys disappeared into the night together." Beth crossed her arms over her chest and made a *tsk-tsk* sound. "So much for that whole 'resisting temptation' thing."

"I don't know how it *happened*!" Ella groaned. "One minute I was sitting there, rejecting all boys, and the next minute . . ." She sighed. "Maybe it was the beer. Well, at least he was cute."

"Are you seeing him again?" Beth asked.

Ella winced. "Unlikely. He barely speaks English."

"So . . ." Beth laughed. "What? You spoke the *language of love*?" She realized that it was exactly the kind of thing George would have said, if he'd been there. She bit her lip.

"Stop. Inigo is an exchange student from Portugal," Ella explained. "And it took about a half hour to get that across."

"His name is *Inigo*?" Beth tried hard not to crack up.

"Well, I think so." Ella shrugged, and a baffled look flitted across her face. "I'm not a hundred percent sure, though. Definitely something foreign."

Beth cackled. "Poor baby," she said. "Maybe you should have asked before you flitted off with him."

Ella frowned and sat up. "I'm not doing this stuff anymore," she said. "I know I said that last night, but I mean it now. It's not worth it." She looked over at Beth, and Beth thought she looked very young all of a sudden. "I want what you have."

"Um, what do I have?" Beth rolled her eyes. "A boyfriend who would rather paint dorms than be with me?"

That was unfair, and moreover, broke her rule about not being a big, fat ol' downer. Beth sighed. What she really needed was something to divert her attention. She had to prove to herself that she could have a good time *without* George. Maybe surfing. She had done some last summer, but still had a way to go before she could ride the waves like that amazing girl who got her arm bitten off by a shark and then competed in some contest the next day.

That was it, Beth decided, momentarily forgetting about Ella's plight. She would transform herself into a surf queen. She would kick George's ass when he visited. It was a great plan. As soon as Ella left, Beth would grab her surfboard and hit the beach.

"I'm serious, Bethy. No more one-night stands with sexy foreigners. I want someone like George," Ella was saying sullenly. "A nice guy. A relationship guy. He's, like, the perfect boyfriend. You're so lucky."

"Yeah, I know," Beth said as tears suddenly sprung to her eyes. She really couldn't believe how much she missed George. She had known it would be bad, but come on, actual *crying*? That wasn't like her at all.

Beth stood and walked over to the window, trying to compose herself before Ella could notice how vulnerable she was.

Outside, their younger cousins, Jordan, Jessi, and Drew, tore around in a game of what looked like sudden-death badminton.

"Is it all right if I crash in your room?" Ella asked, blinking as if her headache had just doubled. "If I go out there, they'll make me play with them and really, I think my head might explode."

"Of course you can," Beth said, keeping her back to Ella. "I'm going down to the beach to surf."

And try to stop moping over said perfect boyfriend.

Surfing actually did the trick. Beth spent that afternoon on her board, and all subsequent afternoons in much the same manner, improving her technique in between text-messaging George. But even after a week, Beth still felt slightly out of shape. Everything ached, and her soreness was really affecting her mojo. One afternoon at the end of June, after she wobbled and missed a completely easy ride, she decided it was time to take a break.

Beth dragged her board across the sand, weaving around the people littering the beach. She spotted noisy families, groups of girls, and packs of teenagers who looked like they might be on the prowl. Music blared from all sides. Beth always liked it when she could hear one song down at the water's edge and follow it all the way to her towel on different radios, all of them tuned to the same station. Down near the pier, the sand was so packed, it was nearly impossible to pick a path through all the towels. Where the Tuttles set up camp, however, it was much less chaotic — just the lifeguard stand down the beach and quiet couples who were dozing off underneath their bright umbrellas.

Beth collapsed on her towel and let the sun tease the cold from her limbs. A light breeze danced along the beach and carried faraway smells of flowers and the rich tang of seaweed. Her skin felt tight from the salt water and the chilly temperature of the ocean. It was still early in the summer, which meant the water was still recovering from the cold Maine winter. The warmest water would be in late August, right when they would have to leave.

Beth moved the fat Jennifer Weiner paperback she had read all of two chapters of so far, off her towel. She pulled her cell phone out of her beach bag and smiled when she saw that there were two text messages waiting for her in her inbox.

DEMAND YOU CALL ME NOW. MIT GEEK GIRLS HAVE ME SURROUNDED. REQUIRE GIRLFRIEND INTERVENTION, George had written.

Beth actually giggled out loud, and covered her mouth with embarrassment. George was the only guy she knew who sent text messages — and e-mails — in complete sentences, with all the words spelled out correctly. And in all caps, no less.

ARE YOU SURFING INSTEAD OF SAVING ME? the second message read.

BEAT THE GIRLS OFF W YOUR PAINTBRUSH. 2 WET 2 CALL. Beth wrote back, still grinning, and slipped the phone back into her bag.

Beth sat up, and pulled her wet blonde hair into a new, tighter ponytail. Last evening, she and Ella had sat out by the picnic tables long after everyone else went to bed, talking about everything and nothing until the fog — the original pea-soup kind Maine was famous for — came up out of nowhere and settled over the yard. But before they went to bed, Ella had been going on about how great it must be to fall in love. Beth had agreed at first, remembering how *inevitable* her and George's coming-together had felt. And how awesome her junior year of high school had been with George there to kiss and cuddle with every afternoon.

But Beth also knew that love was only fun when you knew the outcome. When you were flailing around in the middle of it, it was just like falling off your surfboard every five minutes — it hurt like hell. And it also hurt when you couldn't share all the stupid trivial things of life with the person you loved. Like yesterday, when she found the bluest seashell she'd ever seen. Or the day before, when she saw a five-year-old boy puke chocolate milk shake in front of the Twin Freeze. George was missing everything. And Beth felt like a part of her was missing it, too.

George *was* being wonderfully attentive — texts every hour on the hour, phone calls before they went to bed, and sappy e-mail poems on the weekends (which Beth promised not to forward on to Jamie for critical review). But it still didn't seem to be enough. Beth wanted George there — his physical presence. She craved it. And that awful longing made being in love not so grand, after all.

*　　*　　*

After her short time-out on the beach, Beth resumed her surf-my-blues-away program. An hour later, she was feeling a chill on her skin as she bobbed along. It was way too easy to zone out with all that bright sky and the light reflecting on the waves. She yawned and decided she should call it a day.

Lying on her stomach, Beth paddled herself around and started back toward the beach. She'd only gone a few strokes when she realized, with a little shock, that she was much farther out than she'd meant to go.

Good move, she chided herself. *Getting washed out to sea is not part of the plan.*

She started to paddle harder, but the current was against her, and it seemed to keep sending her farther down shore. Beth wasn't one to panic, but — *hello* — she and George had seen *Open Water* last fall. It was kind of hard not to get mildly freaked.

Think! Beth ordered herself, closing her eyes, but the more she thought, the more panicked she felt. She tried to paddle again, but felt suddenly paralyzed.

At first, Beth thought the buzzing sound was just in her head, and she had gone from panic straight to shock. She thought she was hallucinating, and one step shy from hyper-ventilating, and two steps shy of passing out and drowning.

Lucky for her, the buzzing sound was real.

The Jet Ski came out of nowhere and skidded around to a stop right in front of her. A young man sat astride it like he was floating on the back of a dolphin.

Beth was positive she'd never been so happy to see another person in her life.

"Don't worry," the guy said. "I've got you."

Beth was mesmerized by his regulation red shorts that had ADAM printed on the left leg, and the whistle around his neck. As it turned out, the lifeguards at Pebble Beach really did their job. She'd always thought they were around for show more than anything else.

Adam strapped her board to his Jet Ski, and then helped Beth climb up behind him. She was so not used to feeling like a damsel in distress, but she was too relieved to care.

"Just hold on," he told her, and then he started the motor. Beth wrapped her arms around his waist.

Beth's stomach lurched as the Jet Ski shot across the water. She had to shut her eyes against the wind, so the whole world narrowed down to the muscled back she was holding on to. Beth's heart was still pounding, like she was still stranded out in the center of the ocean. But she wasn't. She'd been saved.

When they got to the beach, Adam helped her get her board to the sand. Calmer now, Beth started to feel embarrassed.

"I'm usually much more careful," she told him, trying not to blush.

He flashed her a big smile. "That current can knock anyone out."

For the first time since he'd rescued her, Beth looked Adam full in the face. He had eyes to match the water and tousled, curly brown hair. He had muscular shoulders and a narrow waist, and all of his skin was a golden bronze. *Not bad-looking,* Beth thought. If she were single, she might almost have a semi-crush on this guy.

"Thanks for saving my ass back there," she said, and was surprised to hear her voice get a little breathy. *All that adrenaline.* "I think I scared myself silly."

"You were in no real danger," Adam told her. He jerked his chin out toward the water. "You eventually would've washed ashore, but over in the next town."

Beth giggled. A girly, Ella giggle that, up until that moment, Beth hadn't thought she was capable of. She had to recover, and fast.

"Well, then," Beth said with a very straight, purposeful face. "Thank you for saving me a long walk home."

"Anytime," Adam replied with a crooked grin.

Beth hoisted up her board, which suddenly felt like it weighed two hundred pounds. She struggled to keep it level, but it just bobbled and ended up hitting her on the head with a loud thud.

"Are you okay?" Adam said with concern. "Do you want to just check in with the first-aid stand?"

"No, no. I'm cool," Beth assured him, tucking the board under her trembling arm. *Just say good-bye and run like the wind,* she thought. "So I guess I'll see you around. Like lifeguarding and stuff." After that lame remark, Beth thought about getting back on her board and letting the current finish the job.

"Sure thing," Adam said, squinting a little bit as he looked at her. "Listen, I'm a decent surfer. Let me know if you ever want a partner, okay?"

"That would be great." *I probably look like I could use one.*

"Excellent." He started back toward the Jet Ski, which was still bobbing with the tide. "Don't get washed away, now," he told her over his shoulder.

"I promise you won't have to rescue me again," Beth told him with a laugh.

"Would be my pleasure," Adam replied.

He waved with one hand, and then climbed back on the Jet Ski. Beth watched him zip away, skimming across the water like a skipping stone.

She trudged up the beach to her towel and dried herself off as well as she could before stepping into her shorts. She felt sandy, salty, and tired right down to the bone. But, as she started up toward the cottages, she was also smiling, for what felt like the first time in days.

7

On the third day of July, Kelsi bundled her three younger cousins into their wet-weather gear, and pulled on her own windbreaker. It was an obnoxiously bright shade of yellow, but the key point was it had a hood, which was essential for fending off Maine thunderstorms. The drenching rain had let up a little bit, so Kelsi just wore her Timberland boots, cutoff Gap jeans, and a purple T-shirt underneath the windbreaker. She was ready.

Once outside, Jordan and Drew took off at a gallop, having been stuck indoors for the entire rainy morning. The rain was washing everything clean, so Kelsi could smell the grass, the dirt, the trees — all of it distinct. She took a deep breath.

"Are we going to walk *all the way* to the farmer's market?" Jessi asked as they started down the dirt road, which, after a whole morning of solid rain, was more like a mud-filled swamp. The littlest of the cousins, Jessi, was wearing a bright pink slicker with a pair of matching galoshes that had Hello Kitty faces on the front of each foot. Kelsi thought she looked adorable, but knew better than to say so.

"It's not far — just down from the pier," Kelsi reminded her. "And we can watch them building the clambake pit on the way."

"I love the clambake," Jessi chirped, clinging tightly to Kelsi's hand.

Every year there was a huge community clambake on the Fourth of July, right down on the beach, near the spot where they'd attended the bonfire a few weeks ago. Kelsi preferred the Tuttles' tradition of eating out in town and then wandering off to see the fireworks, but she loved the way the clambake infused the air all day long with the rich aroma of fire, seaweed, and salt.

Today, the Public Works employees would be out digging the pit and getting everything ready for the celebration. When she'd been younger, Kelsi had been fascinated by the process of digging the hole. She could spend hours watching the men in their bright orange overalls, calling instructions to one another in the Down East accents Kelsi loved to hear and always failed to mimic correctly.

Jordan and Drew ran ahead and jumped in all the puddles while Kelsi and Jessi took the slower route and tried to avoid getting any wetter or muddier. By the time they all reached the farmer's market, Kelsi felt disheveled from trying to keep all the kids from running into every yard on Peachtree Road for a sudden tree-climbing.

The aunts had given Kelsi a detailed list of the things they wanted her to pick up, because Aunt Joanne liked to throw a big brunch on the Fourth. That meant she wanted fresh baked bread, ripe tomatoes, farm-fresh eggs, berries, and other yummy things best found at the farmer's market. Kelsi gave each one of her little cousins a specific job, and then went to pick through the fruit herself. She took her fruits and vegetables seriously, despite the periodic mockery from the rest of her family.

You're not dressing like a hippie anymore, Ella had complained over dinner just last night. *So why do you have to keep eating like one?*

"Well, look at this," said an amused deep voice, interrupting Kelsi's thoughts. "Lucky for you, Kelsi, I decided to remember your name. Because that's the kind of nice guy I am."

Kelsi knew exactly who it was — she recognized that self-satisfied drawl immediately — but she looked up just to make sure.

Sure enough, Tim was lounging against a nearby bin of cucumbers, grinning at her as if he'd known she would turn up. Insufferably blond Tim, looking slightly more rumpled than he had that night at the bonfire. *Rumpled, but still tragically hot,* Kelsi thought. She wondered if it was her lot in life to trip over guys like Tim wherever she went. It made for nice scenery, sure, but why couldn't she ever find a good guy for a change?

"I know what kind of guy you are," Kelsi replied, probably with more bite in her tone than necessary.

"Somehow," Tim said, his grin widening, "that doesn't exactly make me feel better."

"Kelsi! Kelsi!" Jordan came tearing up to her, and rebounded off her legs. Kelsi grabbed him to keep him from falling over. She could just imagine her hyper cousin upending one of the vegetable carts and causing a huge commotion.

"Careful, there," she warned him.

"Two loaves," Jordan said, thrusting the items in question at her. "Am I first? Did I win?"

"You win," Kelsi told him, laughing at his excitement. "You can pick one thing from the Penny Candy, okay?"

"I won!" Jordan whooped, and took off again at top speed.

Kelsi looked back over at Tim and blushed a little when she found him watching her, his hazel eyes still.

"What?" she asked, feeling defensive. "My cousins respond best to bribery."

Tim just kept smiling, which was seemingly motivated by Kelsi's obvious annoyance at his mere presence.

"Why are you here?" she finally asked. "You don't look like the grocery-shopping type."

"You're all about what 'type' I am, aren't you?" he asked, suddenly serious. He stepped around the side of the bin, and Kelsi noticed he was wearing one of the green aprons that indicated he was a working volunteer. *Excuse me?* Frat Boy Tim was also Charity Volunteer Tim? Mr. Football actually planted seeds and grew stuff out of the ground, then donated his time to the community? He cared about doing something that didn't involve running with a ball and colliding with burly guys? Kelsi wasn't used to ever feeling this confused.

"You work here," she said, realizing that she sounded like a complete tool. She felt her face go hot again.

Tim pushed his hair back from his forehead and leaned in close. Kelsi stiffened. She could feel his breath against the damp skin of her neck. Goose bumps popped up across her skin, and she shivered under her windbreaker.

It was the cool, wet weather, she told herself.

"Yup. And I recommend the blueberries," he said, his mouth close to her ear.

"Um . . ." was all Kelsi managed to say.

Tim smiled. He reached over and tapped the tip of her nose with his finger, and then sauntered off, losing himself in the crush of people beneath the big canopy.

Bewildered, Kelsi stood there longer than she should have, looking at him walking away. But this time, *he* was the one who never turned around.

Ella spent the Fourth of July the way it was meant to be spent: lounging on the beach in a tiny bikini, Diet Coke in hand, Bain de Soleil-ing her skin toward a perfect tan.

Yesterday's rain had given way to today's bright heat, and Ella had staked out a perfect spot, where the soft white sand gave way to the harder-packed tidal sand. She could smell the clambake in the air, that hard salt tang that almost made her mouth water, and she didn't even like seafood. Families were setting up elaborate picnics up and down the shore, preparing for the fireworks later that night. Ella's tanning spot was smack in the middle of the commotion. She didn't mind. She liked to be where she could check out the entire beach.

Not that she was checking *anyone* out, Ella reminded herself as she applied another coat of Bain de Soleil. After her wild night with Inigo, she was reformed. No more boys this summer. Period. Even if being boyless was so darn . . . boring.

Ella noticed a set of boys passing by and pretended not to see them enjoy the way she greased up her legs, one shapely calf after the other. The old Ella would have made eye contact, maybe exchanged a few flirtatious words. But the new, post-Inigo Ella remained silent. Which wasn't to say she didn't love the way the tall one swallowed hard when she reclined against her towel.

Ella couldn't help it if she had a certain power. Kelsi was a brilliant student. When Beth performed some athletic feat, everyone talked about her talent. Ella's talent was making boys drool. Everyone had to be good at something.

Ella was turning over when she saw Beth walking up the shore with a lifeguard. As they drew closer, Ella appreciated the way the guy's shoulders moved, to say nothing of the six-pack he was sporting. She debated flinging herself into the water so he could rescue her, but discarded the idea. Daring rescues were romantic, sure, but she didn't like getting wet. All that seaweed and the possibility of jellyfish — yuck.

Beth was deep in conversation with the lifeguard. Her eyes were sparkling in a way Ella hardly recognized. When Beth finally looked away from the lifeguard and waved, Ella wiggled her fingers in reply, but continued to study the lifeguard. He was laughing, and Ella thought he had a familiar-sounding laugh. She tilted her head to the side and considered it. He had that dark curly hair and there was something about the way he —

Ella gasped out loud when she got it.

Pack on a muscled body and skin that actually tanned, and Beth was talking to a clone of George.

It would have been a little creepy if it weren't so funny.

"Hey there," Ella said, smiling her brightest smile, when Beth and the boy arrived at the edge of her towel. "I'm Ella," she told the hot lifeguard.

"Adam," the lifeguard replied. He was even cuter up close. Definitely a movie-star version of George.

"Bethy," Ella pouted. "How dare you hog the attention of the best-looking lifeguard on the beach?"

Beth rolled her eyes, but her cheeks were pink. "Adam's just helping me with my surfing, El. And there are plenty of other lifeguards. Go check out the guys at the station."

"Definitely," Adam said, grinning. Ella noticed, though, that his smile wasn't directed at her, but at Beth. "They could use a distraction. It gets crazy around here on the Fourth."

Ella turned to peer down the beach toward the big white lifeguard station, and shrugged. It seemed awfully far away, across a whole lot of hot sand.

"Are we going out later?" Beth asked, already backing away from Ella's towel.

"That's the plan," Ella said. Beth looked as if she couldn't wait to start her surfing lesson.

"I'll see you back at the cottages," Beth said, and then sauntered off with Adam. Ella smiled. If the situations were reversed, and she was parading around with a sexy lifeguard, Ella knew she certainly wouldn't waste her time on small talk with Beth.

Ella looked back toward the lifeguard station again.

Lifeguards were, by definition, supposed to be in excellent shape. And lifeguarding indicated a certain interest in the welfare of others. That meant they were esentially good guys, right?

So really, she *had* to check it out for herself, just in case her future, serious, long-term boyfriend was there, waiting for her. Ella loosely tied her sarong around her hips. It perfectly matched her fire-engine red bikini. She adjusted her boobs with a few expert pats and she was prepared to go find herself the nice relationship she wanted.

Down near the lifeguard stand, Ella paused to consider her approach. It wasn't quite the all-you-can-eat hottie buffet that Beth had hinted at, but Ella couldn't complain. A tall, broad-shouldered blond guy caught her eye immediately. He had a square jaw and a confident grin that deepened when he saw Ella. She smiled back, but she didn't feel too excited. He was a little too . . . *wholesome.* Besides, Ella liked to be the blonde one in the relationship. It was just a quirk of hers that she couldn't explain.

The lifeguard sitting next to the blond, however, was a different story. At first glance, Ella had dismissed him. He had brown hair and eyes, which Ella liked, but he sat in a sort of careless way that gave her the impression that he didn't think anyone would be paying attention to him. But then he got up and climbed down to the sand in a few easy movements that changed everything Ella had been thinking about him. She took a second look.

He was a puzzle, that was for sure. When he hit the beach,

the easy grace he'd displayed a few moments ago seemed to disappear, and he became a lean, lanky guy with shaggy brown hair. Nothing special.

Except . . . If she looked closely, there was a certain sexy, dark vibe going on that she couldn't resist. Even better, it was clear that he had no idea how cute he was. Ella could spot a winner when she saw one, no matter how awkwardly he carried himself.

She strolled right up to the lanky guy as if she were playing a game of chicken and she knew her opponent would definitely budge first. She made sure he got to enjoy the full effect of her red bikini and her curves. She watched his eyes travel over her and felt a little flicker of something in her heart.

This was the best part of meeting boys. Hands down.

"I'm looking for Adam," she said softly.

"Aren't we all," said the blond from up above. Ella smiled at him, but didn't linger, and quickly looked back at her hottie-in-hiding.

"He's, uh, giving a lesson," Lanky said timidly, as if he couldn't believe Ella was talking to him.

"Oh," Ella said very brightly. "With Beth, right? She's my cousin. We were supposed to meet up. . . ." She broke off, and flashed her sweetest smile at him. "I'm Ella, by the way."

He looked slightly stunned, but Ella took advantage of his reaction by moistening her lips with her tongue and ever-so-casually tousling her hair with her hands while arching her back. And if doing that thrust her breasts out, well, that was okay, too.

"I'm Jeremy," he said, never moving his gaze from her face, which kind of unnerved her. "Adam should be back in about fifteen minutes. You can wait here if you want."

"That sounds like a great idea. Why don't we wait together?"

His wonderfully dark eyes probed hers for a moment, then dropped back over her bikini quickly. Then he looked away and shrugged.

Ella smiled.

Finally, things were looking up.

After the Fourth, Beth's days took on a comfortable routine. In the late morning, she would head down to the beach and work on her surfing alone until Adam took his break. Then he helped her try out different moves. Adam had totally under-sold himself — he wasn't a decent surfer. He was practically a surf Zen master, and he was an even better teacher. Beth felt herself improving by the minute. And her mood was brightening, too.

"I lived in California until I was about twelve," Adam told her on this particularly humid July day, when they were taking a breather. They sat together just above the waterline, watching the waves crash against the sand and then reach for the dunes. "I got into the whole surfing thing out there. The waves are way better there than here on the East Coast."

"Hey, don't disrespect the East Coast," Beth teased, leaning back on her hands.

"Listen," Adam said, turning to look at her, "I love Maine. But the water temperature could stand to be better. I mean, even you were a little blue before."

"I was not!" Beth sat up, pretending to be mad. She'd been cold, true, but they'd been having fun, so who cared? It was like when Beth had been little, and her parents would have to literally drag her, Jamie, Ella, and Kelsi out of the water. The girls had been so hyper and excited that they'd had no idea if they were freezing-cold or not. Surfing with Adam was that kind of fun.

"Hey, it was very becoming," Adam joked.

When their eyes met, Beth felt a warm glow, like the sun was inside her as well as beating down from up above. She couldn't believe that only a few weeks ago, she'd been a mopey, missing-George mess. Funny how making a new friend could cheer her up.

"Want to catch one more wave before you have to get back?" she asked Adam. His breaks always felt way too short.

He was still watching her, a gleam in his blue eyes. Beth felt warmed by that, too.

"I have to get back," he said with regret in his voice. "For some reason, they actually want me to *work*."

"That's crazy!" Beth laughed. For the briefest instant, she wondered if she was flirting. *Nah.* She never flirted.

"Tell me about it." He paused and then shot her a look from beneath the curls that spilled across his forehead. "But maybe we could grab some dinner tonight, if you felt like it."

Beth froze. *Hang on.* Was Adam asking her . . . out?

Taking their friendship from the beach to places where they'd have to wear shoes seemed like a big leap. Adam was her "beach buddy." They existed only in this safe zone. But now Beth felt panicked by Adam's invitation. "Don't swim beyond this point!" she wanted to say.

But maybe she was overreacting. Adam *was* her friend. He'd practically saved her life. Of course she liked him and felt safe with him. It was silly for her to feel like she was betraying George in some way by accepting Adam's invitation. So what if she'd forgotten to check George's text messages that day? It didn't mean anything. She could have a boyfriend and a boy friend at the same time. Couldn't she?

"That would be great," she said at last, trying to play it cool. But then, her smile seemed to get lost in Adam's smile for a long moment.

"Adam's a great guy," Beth told George later that evening as she made her way down the beach, where she was about to meet her favorite new lifeguard. She held her cell phone to her ear and clutched her shoes in her free hand. Beth much preferred to go barefoot, even if the sand was a little chilly in the evening. "Not to mention, he saved my life."

"I owe him, big-time," George said at once. "Anyone who saves you from the clutches of death is a god."

"You would love him," Beth laughed. "I wish you could meet him. I feel like he's practically one of your friends already."

Adam was waiting at the lifeguard stand, leaning against the wooden structure and watching her approach.

"As long as he's funny," George was saying. "I have low-to-zero tolerance for people with no sense of humor."

"He has *exactly* our sense of humor," Beth said, and wondered if she was gushing. "Here, find out for yourself," she added as she approached Adam. She grinned, and handed him her phone. "It's George," she said. He looked at her blankly, and Beth suddenly realized that somehow, in all their conversations, she hadn't even mentioned that she had a boyfriend, let alone one named George. Beth didn't even think that it was possible to flake on such a thing, since she usually referred to George constantly. Didn't she?

After a short, tense pause, Beth added, "He's my boyfriend," hoping to clear up any confusion.

Adam seemed to stiffen, but he already had the cell phone.

"Hi," he said, sounding surprisingly awkward.

Beth furrowed her brow. Surely she'd mentioned George to Adam before. But she wasn't sure she could remember doing it. Her pulse quickened. How could she have missed George so much that she was ready to ship herself to Boston via FedEx, and yet neglect to tell Adam about him at all?

Adam didn't seem to have much to say to George, so Beth took her phone back from him.

"I'll call you later," she said to George.

"Or sooner," George countered. "Don't let Mr. Personality try any funny 'mouth-to-mouth' stuff on you, okay?"

Beth tried to ignore the enormous, if inexplicable, wave of guilt that engulfed her. "Will do," Beth said, laughing. She tucked the phone in her pocket and glanced at Adam.

"So, that was your boyfriend," Adam said, watching her.

Something fluttered in Beth's stomach, but she ignored it. Probably just hunger.

"Yup. Sorry to foist him on you. He's a character."

It seemed like Adam might say something else, but the moment passed. Then Adam gave her his typical warm smile.

"Hungry?" he asked her.

She nodded. "You?"

"I'm so hungry I could eat your shirt," he said as he grabbed the hem of Beth's T-shirt.

It was so something George would have done.

Beth yanked the fabric from Adam's grip and felt a spark when their hands touched. But it didn't mean anything. Adam was just a friend.

George, George, George, she thought.

The next morning, Beth and Ella made their way down to the beach, picking a path across prickly beach grass and pieces of glass. Beth liked the company while she waited for Adam's break, so she could tolerate Ella's newfound interest in all things Jeremy. Apparently, Ella seemed to think that because Beth and Adam were tight, Beth somehow had a window into Jeremy's brain. So Ella asked tons of questions about the shy lifeguard. But Beth couldn't have cared less about Jeremy.

It was the craziest thing, but she couldn't stop thinking

about Adam. Dinner last night had been so much fun that Beth couldn't wait to see him again. She didn't have a *crush* on him or anything, but it would be stupid not to admit that she found his attention the teeniest bit flattering.

"Adam's really funny," Beth told Ella then, as if they'd been talking about Adam all along. "He had me laughing so hard last night I almost choked on my clam sauce. He was one step away from doing the Heimlich and saving my life again."

Ella peered back at Beth over the top of her sunglasses, like some kind of movie star, but said nothing.

"He's been a lifeguard here for a few years now," Beth continued. "I can't believe it — I mean, it's so weird that I never saw him before this summer."

"Weird," Ella echoed, her tone slightly wry.

"He showed me this really cool new way to balance on my board," Beth chattered on. She didn't know why Ella was being so quiet, but she didn't care. "It's so simple, but I never would have thought of it on my own. He's an amazing surfer."

"The most amazing thing about Adam," Ella said, shoving her sunglasses back up on her nose, "is how much he reminds me of this other guy we know."

Beth wrinkled her nose in confusion. "He does?"

"You don't see it?" Ella shook her head. "Come on, Bethy. I'm not exactly Ms. Perceptive, but I noticed it right off."

"You *are* perceptive," Beth said. She frowned at Ella as they reached the last turn of the path that cut through the dunes to the water. "But who do you think he looks like?"

"Take a moment and think *real hard*," Ella said through an

amused smirk. Seagulls jeered at one another overhead, and Beth shrugged and wiped at the dried salt on her face.

"I give up," she said.

"Well," Ella began, sounding particularly pleased with herself, "he could be George's brother. Not his identical twin. Maybe fraternal."

Beth went very still. "Adam isn't anything like George." Even though, last night, she'd told George that they had a similar sense of humor. But so what?

Ella was on a roll. "And that laugh? Hello — *totally* George," she said, shaking her head. "Trust you to go out and find a carbon copy. I think I'll call him G-2 from now on."

Beth didn't respond. She was suddenly acutely aware of how hot the sand beneath her feet felt. She picked up her pace so much, she shot by Ella altogether, each grain of sand embedding itself in her feet along the way.

Ella dressed carefully for the night's activities. The cousins were all going out to eat at the Lobster Shack, the new dinner joint in town, where, according to Beth, G-2 was supposed to turn up with the delicious Jeremy. Ella was wearing a skimpy pink miniskirt she'd picked up at Urban Outfitters with a pair of pink round-toed Steve Madden heels that would have looked dangerous in New York City and were — at best — highly inappropriate for a beach town. She'd chosen her strappiest black tank top — courtesy of Abercrombie — because it clutched her breasts lovingly and made her waist look practically nonexistent.

"How do you walk in those shoes?" Kelsi asked, as Ella — who believed in mind over matter when it came to stiletto heels — sauntered down the dirt road like it was her own personal runway.

Ella just smiled mysteriously. There was no point in

explaining the art of walking in heels to her boring sister — it was all about leaning back.

"I'm impressed," Beth chimed in, linking her arm through Kelsi's and observing Ella.

Ella noticed that Beth wasn't wearing her jogging clothes tonight. She'd opted for what looked like Levi's, a cute little T-shirt that said ADULT SWIM on the front, and, if Ella wasn't mistaken, lip gloss.

Very interesting, Ella thought, but then she had to concentrate on not tripping over an exposed root instead of Beth's fashion choices. That was the problem with being known for inappropriate shoes: People would never let you hear the end of it if you actually exhibited even the teeniest problem with them. Ella always had to pretend that the five-inch heels she sometimes wore didn't hurt a bit when in actuality they were rubbing her skin raw.

When they got into town, Kelsi and Beth headed straight toward the Lobster Shack, but Ella found herself far more interested in the flashing lights and music coming from another new Pebble Beach venue, the Lighthouse.

"Have you guys checked this place out yet?" she asked.

"You can't get in there unless you're twenty-one," Kelsi said firmly, sounding very "big sister."

"Whatever," Ella replied breezily. "Don't underestimate me, Kels."

"Trust me," Kelsi said to Ella. "They won't let you in."

Ella always enjoyed a challenge, so she blew a kiss at her

sister and Beth and headed straight for the Lighthouse. She could meet up with them — and Jeremy — later. As she approached, she could see the bouncers already sizing her up. She ignored them and concentrated on the music she could hear from outside. Whenever the door opened, she liked what she could see of the wooden and red interior. It looked exciting and *adult*, the sort of place cool people would go to drink whiskey or something. She imagined it was the kind of place guys like hot alterna-rockers would hang out in. Ella got a little closer so she could get a better look.

"Don't even bother, little girl," the bigger of the two bouncers growled.

Ella wasn't fazed at all and gave him a sultry wink. Flirting with thirty-year-olds didn't intimidate her in the least. She produced a cigarette from her bag and put it to her lips. The bouncer just stared at her. "Come on," Ella wheedled. "You won't let me in *and* you won't give me a light? Is anyone that mean?"

The bouncer shook his head, but he laughed and dug a lighter from his pocket.

"Oh boy. You're trouble," he told her.

"Whenever possible," Ella agreed.

She gave him another big smile, and made sure she wiggled her hips as she turned and walked away. She took a drag of her cigarette, and then decided she didn't really want it and flicked it away. She was trying to figure out a better way to get inside the Lighthouse — and Ella had no doubt that she would find a way in, eventually — when she saw a familiar figure walking toward her. *Jeremy*.

Things couldn't have worked out better. Jeremy was right there in front of her, and she didn't have to deal with any of his lifeguard friends or anyone else. His attention would be where it belonged: on her and her alone.

"Hey there," she said, stepping boldly in front of him. He looked surprised, as if he hadn't recognized her from far off, which Ella dismissed as unlikely.

"Ella," he said in his usual wobbly voice. It was almost as if he were scared of her. She dismissed that, too.

"Jeremy," she replied, helping herself to his arm and leaning into him. "What perfect timing. I was just wishing that I had someone to walk with me."

All Jeremy could do was fidget and shift his weight around uncomfortably. Ella loved the way his shaggy hair got even messier when he raked his hand through it. He was truly the cutest geek she had ever laid eyes — and hands — on.

"I'm going to the Lobster Shack," she said, trying to coax him out of his shell. "Were you on the way there?"

Jeremy scratched his face. "Uh, not really, no."

"Well, I thought you were going to meet up with us for something to eat."

"Yeah, I was . . . but now, I, like, can't," Jeremy stammered.

Ella found herself smiling at him. Could she really make someone this nervous? It was pretty flattering.

"Why not?" she asked.

Jeremy took a deep breath. "I just found out that there's a John Cusack doubleheader down at the Royale Theatre. You know, the one at the other end of town?"

"The one that never has any good movies?" Ella asked dubiously.

"No, they do," Jeremy told her. "They're showing *Better Off Dead* and *One Crazy Summer,*" he added. As he talked, he got more and more animated and much less awkward. It was like when he'd climbed out of the chair. When he forgot to be self-conscious, he had the kind of vibe that Ella adored. "I mean, *Better Off Dead* is a work of genius, really, but there's something to be said for *One Crazy Summer,* too." He seemed to realize he was rambling, and he smiled, more at himself than at Ella. "You're not a John Cusack fan?" he asked.

"Of course I am," Ella said. "I saw that thing at the motel, with the serial killer."

"Early John Cusack," Jeremy clarified, still wearing that adorable smile. "It's a whole different thing. He was, like, his own genre."

He suddenly seemed so confident that Ella was dying to kiss him.

"I have an idea," Ella murmured, leaning a little bit closer, so her breasts brushed up against him. "Why don't I join you? We can watch the movie, or we can . . ."

Jeremy looked at her for a long moment, and his eyes widened, as if he couldn't believe what she was suggesting. But instead of smiling, as Ella hoped he would, Jeremy stepped back and put a Texas-size chunk of space in between them. Then he moved his arm so Ella let her hands drop away. This was *not* the usual boy reaction to her. Ella was completely stunned.

"Thanks, but I'm okay going alone," Jeremy said softly, his face dark red.

Ella was actually embarrassed — imagine that — when she saw the red blotches on Jeremy's cheekbones as he stepped around her as if she were a pit bull about to attack.

Jeremy reverted to his awkwardness. "I . . . uh . . . really should, you know, get going. The movie . . . um . . . starts in . . . like, ten minutes." Then he turned and bolted. Ella was left standing on the street, speechless.

A group of guys walked by her and there were a few whistles, but Ella was too out of sorts to appreciate it. Much less look to see if any of them were hot.

What the hell just happened? Ella wondered, annoyed. She turned and started walking toward the Lobster Shack, but the truth was, she wasn't really in the mood for fried food and a jukebox. Nor was she up for the thumping music of the Lighthouse. All she wanted was for Jeremy to change his mind and come running back. She waited several moments for that to happen, and then gave up. This was unprecedented. A guy actually bailed on her. Was she in some kind of parallel universe where her life just completely sucked?

An angry surge suddenly charged through Ella. She'd just have to march into the Lobster Shack, find other boys to adore her, and have a great time *without* stupid Jeremy — a great time she fully intended his friends to see and report back to him.

Just outside the restaurant, Ella felt her cell phone vibrate in the tiny pocket of her skirt. She didn't recognize the incoming phone number, so she went directly to the text message. Her stomach clenched in confusion.

U BACK YET? NEED 2 C U

But it was the name at the bottom that sent Ella's head spinning:

PETER.

"Your cousin seems into my friend Jeremy," Adam said to Beth as they left the Lobster Shack, trailing far behind Ella, Kelsi, and Adam's other lifeguard friends. There was a slight chill in the air, but Beth found it invigorating.

"What makes you say that?" she asked. Beth had been paying close attention to the cadence in Adam's voice and scrutinizing his face ever since Ella had called him that ridiculous G-2 nickname. She still didn't see the resemblance.

"Well, I think it's because she told me that she was going to make Jeremy her boyfriend, whether he liked it or not." Adam snickered.

See, that sounded nothing like George! Beth told herself. Okay, even if there was a slight similarity, which there wasn't, a lot of people sounded the same when they laughed. It wasn't like there were so many different ways to laugh. You only had so many options.

"Ella's kind of . . . direct," Beth explained. "It's part of her charm."

"So," Adam said, turning so he could look at her as they walked. "What do you do for fun during the summer? You know, besides get your surf on?"

Beth felt suddenly flustered by Adam's attention.

"This and that," Beth replied. "What do you do?"

"My friend Ben throws a few parties every summer," Adam said. "They're fun, but they always get a little crazy. He lives in one of those big houses up on Cranberry Lane." Adam shook his head. "I just don't get why you would come all the way to the beach, and then spend your time sitting in a pool in your backyard." He sounded personally offended by the notion.

"The best thing about Cranberry Lane is that all the pools are laid out in practically a straight line in all the backyards," Beth told him, gesturing with her hands. "Perfect for late-night pool-hopping."

"I like the sound of that," Adam said. They had stopped walking, and were just outside the ice-cream shop, the Twin Freeze. "Are you talking about the usual form of pool-hopping, or something more extreme, like skinny-dipping?"

"Skinny-dipping?" Beth repeated. Suddenly, a memory from last summer flashed through her mind. George had gone skinny-dipping with some random girl and Beth, insanely jealous, had stolen his clothes. She and George had wound up running through the woods — he naked — and later on, kissing for the first time. For some reason, even though that was one of her favorite stories, she didn't share it with Adam, who seemed to recoil whenever she said George's name. And anyway, that was private stuff, between her and George.

"Do you like skinny-dipping?" Adam asked. When Beth nodded, he said quietly and very deliberately. "I bet you look even more beautiful swimming underneath the moonlight."

His words hung there, soft but unmistakable, in the dark between them. *Did he really just call me beautiful?* Beth wished that this was one of those yellow-flag moments in football when you could ask the referee to review the play. Since that wasn't going to happen, she felt the next best thing to do was to deflate the moment before it went somewhere dangerous.

"Adam?" Beth began in a wary voice. *Oh my God, why am I trembling?*

"I know, you have a boyfriend," Adam said, looking down at his New Balances. "The great ones always do."

Beth cast around for something to say. *Shit.* Did Adam like her? More important, did *she* like him? This was spinning out of control. Beth enjoyed Adam's attention, but she knew that if she fueled this fire, she'd really get burned. How could she cool things off with him? Then an idea shot into Beth's head.

"But I happen to know a great one who isn't taken," she said suddenly.

Adam blinked. "You do?"

"Uh-huh. My cousin," Beth said, excited by her stroke of brilliance.

"Um, Ella's nice and all," Adam said, "but she's not really my type and —"

Beth rolled her eyes. "Not Ella. Her sister, Kelsi."

74

It made sense. Kelsi deserved a cool guy, and she was smart, fun, and pretty in a really natural way. Adam would go for her.

"You want me to date your cousin," Adam finally said, like he couldn't quite grasp it.

"Why not?" Beth replied. "She's really cute, and supersmart."

"Beth," he said, sighing heavily. "I don't think that would be a good idea."

"This is where *you* have to trust me," Beth said, unsure of herself, but trying to focus on the task at hand. "You know about surfing, and I know about . . . matchmaking."

Adam's mouth curved up in a crooked grin. "Matchmaking? Ah, you mean working on the assembly line, making sure all the little pieces of wood have round red tops at the end. Got it."

"Smart-ass," Beth said under her breath, while Adam laughed at his own display of wit.

"Okay, B. I'll think about it." He said at last.

Beth noticed two things as Adam took her hand and led her into the Twin Freeze: that she wasn't sure she wanted Adam to date Kelsi, and she loved that he had said she was beautiful.

Later that night, Beth curled up on her bed and cradled her cell phone next to her ear. She and George had been talking for an hour, catching up on the day's activities. George told her some story about falling off a ladder into a vat of paint thinner and how he was high all afternoon because he didn't change out of his fume-infested clothes. Beth laughed at the funny things he said, but there was a part of her that wasn't paying attention. Her conversation with Adam was plaguing her.

"So, what's up with you?" George asked after a moment of silence.

"Uh . . . nothing really. Just hanging out," she replied.

"So, any catfights yet?" George asked.

"No, everyone's fine."

"Damn. I was hoping for some girl-on-girl action."

"Sorry, George. Just good old-fashioned girl–guy relationships going on here." Beth said.

"I feel bad for the poor suckers who get trapped by the Tuttle cousins," George replied. "Who are the latest victims?"

"Actually, I'm trying to set up Adam and Kelsi," Beth said brightly, hoping that this would dismiss any possible thought in George's mind that she had more than friendly feelings for Adam.

"Check it out," George said, sounding pleased. "My best girl is playing Cupid. How completely un-you."

"Well, it's true. I, Beth Tuttle, am now an expert on true love and happily ever after," she joked as she stretched out across her bed.

"I can't argue with that," George said softly. "I miss you, Bethy."

"I miss you, too," she said.

Beth felt a sense of calm come over her. It felt like she was taking a warm bath and all of her worries and anxieties were being completely washed away. She simply loved George like no one else. How could she have forgotten this feeling while she was flirting with Adam? Everything seemed trivial and meaningless compared to the connection she shared with George.

There were a few seconds of silence. Beth closed her eyes and searched her heart.

"I think," she said quietly, "that when you come up here, it's time."

"Wow," he whispered, instantly knowing what she meant. "You mean . . . ?"

"I want to," Beth said. She cleared her throat and sat up. "I want to have sex. With you."

"Are you sure?" he asked. "For real, this time? You might have blocked it out, but believe me, I remember the Valentine's Day incident."

Beth giggled. "I said I was sorry, like, five million times! And I promise no more candles that close to the bed."

"Or, my personal favorite, what I like to think of as The Great Condom Disaster?" George asked with a grunt that sent Beth into a laughing spell. "You can laugh all you want, Bethy, but I was the one who was chased out of Walgreens by my mother's best friend. Who, by the way, *still* likes to bring it up whenever she sees me, *particularly* around my mom."

"Listen, George. I don't want to wait anymore." Beth had never been more sure about anything in her life. "And what better place for it to happen than here in Pebble Beach?"

"You're right," George said. They were both quiet for a minute, and then both of them started laughing at the same time. "That got serious, huh?"

"I guess it *is* pretty serious," Beth said.

"I love you, Bethy," George said softly, exactly the way he said it when he was nuzzling her neck.

"I love you, too," Beth said, and if she closed her eyes again, she could imagine him right there next to her, where he belonged.

From: jtuttle@amherst.edu
To: bethtuttle34@aol.com
Subject: Re: The Usual Shenanigans!!!

Beth,

That story about your first night at the pier was so funny I think I broke a rib from laughter. (They love me here in my dorm — I'm the crazy laughing girl who never leaves her computer.) Maybe you should be the writer in this family. In fact, considering the critique I just got (my hot professor isn't quite so hot when he's ripping my story apart for its "sophomoric" style — OUCH!), you guys should come take my place here. And when ARE you guys coming?? That first weekend in August is best for me.

Back to Pebble Beach intrigue: Tell me the truth — Ella's hook up wasn't *really* named Inigo, was he???

You're just making that up to get a cheap *Princess Bride* laugh. (It worked, you'll be happy to know!!) And don't tell me Kelsi's still moping over that musician from last summer. SUCH A LOSER. He was never good enough for her anyway. Pebble Beach has boys everywhere — she just needs to find the right one.

Most crucially: Who's this Adam guy, the surf hunk? You were suspiciously casual about him in that last e-mail. Too bad for you, Ella's filled me in (I quote):

who cares about some stupid fling ask beth about her new boyfriend G-2 — total clone of the original — luv luv luv E

You're so busted, Beth Tuttle. Tell me everything!
Love, Jamie

Beth went for a jog later that afternoon, taking one of the trails that wound through the woods. Usually, Beth loved to run in and out of the trees — the pine needles carpeted the earth beneath her feet and everything smelled like bark and flowers. But today she was in a bad mood.

Maybe it was Jamie's e-mail. Beth didn't like the fact that Ella was so obsessed with the Adam–G-2 thing. Which wasn't even a *thing*, she reminded herself, working her legs harder.

After all, he and Kelsi had hit it off when she'd introduced them at the arcade a few nights ago. The two of them had started to talk and laugh while Beth got involved with a game of Ms. Pac-Man, expecting to feel all satisfied that her match-making had worked. Beth tried to concentrate on the glowing pellets on the screen, but every time she heard Adam crack a joke and Kelsi's easy, natural giggle, she gripped the joystick in a choke hold that would have killed a small animal.

Forget satisfied. Beth felt sick. Every time she glanced over and saw Adam and Kelsi smile, Beth felt like she was hooked up to some type of medieval torture device — the one that painfully stretches you out in all different directions. A kind of feeling that was eerily familiar. She'd sucked down about five Cokes before she recognized what was happening — and when she'd felt it before.

It was exactly the way she'd felt last summer, when she had realized that she was in love with George.

She ran the last part of the trail at full tilt, bursting through the trees and out into the sunlight along Peachtree Road. She slowed when she hit the sidewalk, and took big, deep breaths, like she could flush her conflicted feelings away by filling her lungs with the fresh morning air.

Obviously, she told herself sternly, she was just missing George, so she was trying to re-create how she had felt last summer. That had to be it.

Beth wiped at the sweat on her forehead, and started back toward the cottages, feeling no more settled than she had before.

When she heard her phone ringing from the pocket of her shorts, she ignored it. She knew that it was George calling again, and she didn't feel like talking to him. He would know something was wrong just from her voice. He would want to talk about it and that was the *last* thing Beth wanted to do.

Then it struck her — Beth had finally encountered one topic that she couldn't ever share with George. Her phone beeped, indicating that he'd left a message.

Why am I avoiding him? Beth wondered. She'd ignored his cell from earlier in the day as well. Was she not in love with George anymore? Was that crazy?

The paved road ended, and Beth turned off onto the dirt track that led up to the cottages. The trees closed in around her, high and fresh-smelling, and she could hear insects hum and the leaves shift and murmur far above. Up ahead, she made out the raised voices of her younger cousins and the clank of plates and cutlery as the Tuttles prepared for their nightly barbecue-fest. It was dinnertime already?

She felt like bursting into tears.

"Beth!" her father called from where he stood at the barbecue. "You almost missed dinner!"

"I lost track of time," Beth murmured.

Beth's dad — always the most enthusiastic griller in the family — dispensed hamburgers and hot dogs, and a few steaks for the grown-ups. Beth loaded up her plate with cheeseburger fixings and a lot of lettuce she didn't actually want.

"You don't want any potato salad?" her mom asked, eyeing Beth's plate doubtfully. "I made the kind you like, with the new potatoes and bacon."

"I'm fine with this," she told her mother, and smiled as if she wasn't feeling horrible.

"Rabbit food's not your style, Bethy," her dad chimed in. "Let me know when you want a second burger."

Ignoring them, Beth headed over to the picnic table traditionally reserved for the older cousins. The younger kids were sitting with Uncle Carr and Aunt Claire, fighting over the amount of vegetables they'd been served, as well as the score of a parent versus kids badminton match.

"You cheat!" Drew was accusing Aunt Claire. "Everyone knows you do!"

"Eat your tomatoes," Uncle Carr retorted.

Beth expected to see both her cousins, but only Kelsi was around. Beth felt a lump in her throat when she swallowed.

"I went down to the beach to look for you," Kelsi said when Beth neared the table. "I'm going out with that friend of yours tonight."

Adam. There he was again. Looking down at Kelsi, Beth felt scraggly in her sweaty tank and shorts.

"Um, really?" Beth asked then, before the silence dragged on too long. "That's so cool!" She thought her voice sounded brittle and fake, but Kelsi didn't seem to notice.

"Yeah," Kelsi said, and shrugged. "It should be fun." She patted the bench next to her and Beth took a seat. "I have no idea what to wear. Wanna help me after dinner?"

You've got to be kidding me, Beth thought.

"Well, uh . . ." She felt like her tongue was made of glue. "I promised George I'd call him, so . . ." Beth lied. "We're going to eat dinner together."

Kelsi smiled. "Aw . . ." She made a shooing motion with her hand. "Go on, then. Go be cute. I'll dress myself."

Beth walked into the house, up to her room, and sank

down on the bed. She set her plate on the dresser, not in the least bit hungry. Her phone rang again, echoing loudly in the quiet room. George. Beth let it ring, and then listened while it made another soft voice-mail beep.

She knew he was waiting for her. But Beth also knew she couldn't bring herself to call George back. Not when she was feeling so torn between him . . . and Adam.

12

The bowling alley was alive with flashing lights and the crash and thunder of balls rolling down the shiny, waxed lanes. Outkast was blaring from the speakers, while kids heckled one another over sloppy techniques and low scores. Kelsi could feel the energy zing through her when she and Adam entered all the chaos.

"I don't remember the last time I went bowling," Kelsi said, grinning at him. "I think I was ten and at someone's birthday party."

"I can't tell you what great news that is," Adam said, fastening the laces on his rented shoes. "Because I'm terrible. I was afraid you were going to kick my ass and I'd have to sit here and be a good loser."

"You're not a good loser?" Kelsi asked, trying to size him up.

"Of course not." Adam flashed his slow smile. "There's no such thing."

Kelsi laughed at that as she followed Adam through the crowd and down to lane 13. She caught sight of herself in one of the mirrors along the wall and ran a reflexive hand over her hair. She'd borrowed one of Ella's Juicy tank tops to wear with a pair of khaki cargo capris from Anthropologie. She liked the result — sort of trendy and earthy all at once.

As they got settled in their cozy little booth, Adam set about programming their names into the machine while Kelsi tested the weight of different bowling balls. One was so heavy she nearly dropped it on her foot. Another had finger holes so slender she was afraid she'd have to wear the thing as an accessory for the rest of her life.

"So you must be psyched for college, right?" Adam asked.

"I guess," Kelsi said, weighing a purple ball in her right hand. "It's just weird to have no idea what might happen next in your life."

Adam nodded. He was seventeen, Kelsi knew, so he wasn't going to college for another year. She'd never been out with a younger guy. "I know what happens next," he said. He indicated the lane in front of her with a flourish. "You get to go first."

Kelsi decided the ball in her hand would do well enough, and stepped up to the end of the lane. She frowned at the pins ahead of her. She had no idea what she was doing, so she snuck a look out of the corner of her eye at the overly serious girl in the next lane, who wore this robotic contraption on her arm and appeared to be performing at championship levels. Kelsi gulped hard and took another look at the pins, wound up, and threw the ball as hard as she could.

The deep purple ball hit the lane with a heavy thud, and then rolled directly into the gutter.

"Well, whaddya know," Kelsi said, laughing as she turned. "I suck."

Adam smiled too quickly, and Kelsi got the feeling that he'd been miles away — preoccupied with something. She flopped down into the seat as he searched for a ball, and watched as he selected a glossy black one.

Kelsi wasn't above a little ogling, and Adam was definitely worth the look. He wasn't classically good-looking, but his features seemed to work together in a way that made him kind of sexy even when he was doing something mundane like winding up to bowl.

But while Kelsi could appreciate the sexy vibe Adam had going on, she wasn't drawn to it the way she thought she should be. She remembered feeling so into Peter that when he'd touched her, she'd felt it all over her body. And with Adam, she just didn't feel that rush, despite the fact she wanted to. Really, *really* wanted to. On paper, he was the guy for her in every way. Funny. Smart. Nice. Completely *not* an asshole.

She mulled it over as they played out their game, competing for the worst score of all time. Kelsi won — in the sense that she lost, horribly — but only because Adam hit a sudden and inexplicable strike streak.

"It just doesn't make any sense," Adam complained, shaking his head.

"Don't tell me you're a sore winner, too!" Kelsi teased.

Adam laughed, and when his eyes danced, Kelsi felt a spark. Maybe she was putting too much pressure on the whole thing — after all, it couldn't be healthy to be thinking *Will he be the one I fall for and lose my virginity to?* every thirty seconds. And Kelsi had to admit that's what she'd been doing. But try as she might, she just couldn't picture herself in Adam's arms that way.

Adam raised an eyebrow at Kelsi. "Want to go again?"

"Um?" Kelsi asked. "Oh, you mean bowl?" *Not sex, you moron!*

"That's what we've got to work with." His smile was warm and inviting, even infectious.

"Then let's do it," Kelsi said.

"Great. I'll buy us another game. Be right back."

She liked the way he moved as he made his way back toward the counter. And there was that smile. And really, he was so —

Kelsi jumped when a male body plunked down in the seat next to her.

"Oh!" she said, sitting up. Whatever she had been thinking about completely disappeared when she saw that the person sitting in Adam's seat was not Adam, but Tim. The last time she'd seen him had been at the farmer's market right before the Fourth of July.

He wasn't wearing anything particularly exciting — just a T-shirt thrown over some ratty old jeans — and yet, of course, he was the sort of guy who made something so basic look mouthwatering.

"You keep turning up," she said, and not in a welcoming way. Tim merely grinned and settled back in the chair he'd commandeered.

"Happens so often, we might as well make a plan for it to happen again," he said.

"Or not," Kelsi retorted.

"Is that your phone?" Tim asked. As Kelsi nodded, he reached across the table, scooped it up, and started pushing buttons.

"Um, could you get your hands off my personal property?" Kelsi demanded, but she made no move to reach for the phone. Instead, she just watched his very long, slender fingers dance around on the keypad.

"There," Tim said after a moment.

"What did you do?" Kelsi didn't take the phone back when he tried to hand it to her. She just stared at it warily as if it were a detonator to an atomic bomb.

"What, are you worried about cooties?" Tim teased her.

Irritatingly, Kelsi felt herself blush. She snatched the phone out of his hand and examined it.

"I put my number in your phone book," Tim said with an

all-too-charming chuckle. "So you can call and ask me out. That's Tim with a T."

"Uh-huh." Kelsi rolled her eyes. "I'll be sure to do that."

"I also called myself, so now I have your number, too," Tim continued happily. "See how easy that was?"

"We're not going on a date," Kelsi told him. She had to struggle to remain stern. "Ever."

"I don't think that's entirely true," Tim replied, unfazed.

Kelsi noticed that the more she tried to put him off, the more confident he seemed. Like he knew something she didn't. How delusional was he?

"Just forget it," Kelsi said, wishing she didn't always sound like a cranky five-year-old around him.

"Why?" Tim asked, studying her curiously.

Kelsi was totally caught off guard. "I don't have time to date." Wow, that was the best she could do? "This is really a busy summer. Uh . . . I'm taking a road trip —"

"I love road trips," Tim interrupted. "Some of my friends consider me an absolute road trip must-have. Kind of like a survival kit."

"Good for you." Kelsi shook her head again, trying to convey her disdain.

"Where are you going?" he asked.

"Does it even matter?"

"Well, we *could* get all philosophical here . . ." He grinned.

Kelsi was at her wit's end with this guy. "Ugh. We're going to Amherst, if you must know. Okay?"

"Amherst?"

That apparently got his attention.

"My cousin is in a summer writing program there," Kelsi said coolly.

Suddenly, Tim looked way too excited.

"What a coincidence," he said. "When are you going?"

"The first weekend in August," Kelsi said. "Why do you care?"

"As a matter of fact," Tim said, "I have to be at U Mass that weekend for an orientation thing. It's obviously fate. We should road-trip together."

Kelsi burst out laughing. *Fate?* Jock Boy was too much. People in the booth next to them turned around to see why Kelsi was cracking up.

"It'll be awesome," Tim said, as if Kelsi hadn't just mocked him. "I realize you somehow don't see what a great guy I am, which I admit hurts pretty bad. But a few hours in the car with me and you'll change your mind. I guarantee it."

"You really are insane." Kelsi was still laughing. "And there's no way I'm letting insanity into my car."

"Then we're on!" Tim grinned and stood up. "I'm sure you'll call me soon, so we can talk about it then. Finalize plans, make a driving schedule, whatever."

"Tim," Kelsi said, frowning up at him, "you can't just invite yourself —"

"Oh look," Tim said, ignoring her. "I think your date is coming back. And here I thought you didn't have time for dating."

Kelsi should have been furious. She knew that she should have yelled at Tim, or stood up and very matter-of-factly explained that she wouldn't allow him to just railroad her, but for some odd reason, she didn't do anything like that. She just watched as Tim turned and sauntered back into the crowd.

"Who was that?" Adam asked, putting two sodas down on the little console.

"Oh," Kelsi said, feeling somewhat light-headed. In her snipe-fest with Tim, she'd actually *forgotten* about Adam. How was that possible? She peered into the crowd, but was unable to see Tim anymore. "Just some guy I met earlier in the summer."

Just some guy I met earlier in the summer, Kelsi thought later, trudging up the dirt road and listening to the sound of the surf, carried up on the night breeze from the beach. *Some guy I don't even like!*

Yet, when she replayed tonight in her mind, Kelsi realized that she had more fun disliking Tim than she had hanging out with Adam. If she couldn't fall for a great guy like Adam, then something was seriously defective in her. What more could she possibly want? Adam was so polite he hadn't even tried to kiss her. Which was a good thing, wasn't it? It meant he probably respected her. More so than, say, Peter the Jerk, who had been groping her practically within moments of saying hello.

Or maybe he just wasn't that into her.

Or maybe she was just overanalyzing, an especially bad idea in the pitch dark. Kelsi had to walk more by memory than by sight, which involved a lot of stepping gingerly. Every time she found herself alone on the dirt road, she was convinced she would get lost in the woods forever. One of these days, she was going to have to remember to bring along a flashlight. Eventually, she came out into the clearing where the Tuttle cottages stood together, lights shining from within.

Kelsi was headed toward her cottage when she heard a noise she couldn't immediately place, a rhythmic *thunk*. She squinted into the darkness of the yard and saw a figure over by the picnic tables, playing with the ersatz tetherball set Uncle Gary had fashioned out of a pole and a tennis ball that afternoon.

As she got closer, Kelsi saw that it was Beth. A fleece pulled over her jeans, she was slamming the ball with a Ping-Pong paddle, looking pissed.

"Hey," Kelsi said.

Beth glanced up, and Kelsi swore she stiffened.

"It's you," Beth said. She whacked the ball and then whacked it harder as it whizzed by, so it went even faster. "So how was it?"

"What?" Kelsi was trying to process why Beth seemed so cold.

"Your date," Beth said. *Thunk.* "Did you have fun?" *Thunk.* "Was there kissing?" *Thunk.* And then another, even harder *thunk.*

"I'm not sure the tennis ball can take all the abuse," Kelsi murmured.

"Sorry," Beth muttered. She caught the ball in her hand as it went by. Then she dropped it, so it thudded against the pole and danced there on the end of the rope.

"Are you okay?" Kelsi ventured. "You seem . . . I don't know . . . really mad about something."

Beth hugged herself and rocked back on her heels. She didn't look at Kelsi.

"Things are kind of weird with George," she said after a moment.

"Weird how?" Kelsi asked. She rubbed her hands along her arms, wishing she'd gone for warmth rather than cuteness when she'd selected Ella's Juicy tank. It had been fine in the bowling alley, and even okay when she'd been walking. But standing still in the Maine night air, she was shivering.

"I don't know." Beth looked away, out toward the beach, as if she could see the horizon at midnight in the black night. "I guess I've been busy, and he's freaking out because he can't talk to me every five seconds." She scrunched her shoulders up beneath her fleece. "I wanted us to spend the summer together, but he wanted to do his whole MIT thing. And now suddenly *I'm* the bad guy because I'm not available every single time he calls." Her voice rose as she spoke. Kelsi reached over and put a hand on Beth's arm to soothe her.

"You guys have been together a long time," Kelsi said. "And you were friends for even longer. This is just a phase, you know?"

"It's a pretty upsetting phase." Beth sighed. "And now I

can't go on the road trip with you guys, because apparently that's the only weekend he can come up. I talked to him tonight and he told me."

"So we'll reschedule," Kelsi said immediately.

"We can't," Beth said in a low voice. "That's the best weekend for Jamie. She e-mailed me today. You guys should go. I should be here for George. . . ." She trailed off.

"It's all going to be okay," Kelsi assured her. "It's just the distance that's making you feel weird about George. You're not used to spending so much time away from him."

"True," Beth admitted. She smiled slightly, then looked closely at her cousin.

"But you had a good time, right?" she asked. "With Adam?"

"I did," Kelsi said. She suddenly didn't want to tell Beth what she'd been thinking about Adam versus Tim. It seemed so important to Beth that she and Adam hit it off — maybe because things were so strange with George lately. No need to make her feel like her matchmaking wasn't working out on top of everything else.

"He's such a great guy," Beth said, and sounded sad.

If only I liked him, Kelsi thought. But she wanted to make Beth feel better, so she didn't tell her the truth.

"Yeah," Kelsi said. "He's exactly what I've been looking for."

13

When Ella's phone beeped for the second time, she noticed that Kelsi looked up from the morning paper she'd spread out in front of her on the kitchen table. Ella froze with her hand on the coffeepot, convinced that Kelsi could somehow look into the pocket of her yellow terrycloth bathrobe and tell who was texting her. Or somehow hear, by the tone of the beep or something, that it was Peter. For the fifth time in four days.

"You are entirely too popular," Kelsi said. She smiled so affectionately that Ella actually felt queasy. Kelsi made it worse by getting up and crossing over to Ella to ruffle her hair.

"How many times do I have to tell you not to touch my hair?" Ella asked, hoping she sounded less tense than she felt.

Kelsi grimaced. "Okay, prima donna. I'm getting in the shower," she announced. "Yesterday you used up all the hot water."

"I'm sorry," Ella said. She must have sounded more

contrite than she should have, because Kelsi shot a quizzical look her way.

"It's okay, El," she said. "I can handle cold water."

With another get-a-grip-you-lunatic look, Kelsi padded out of the kitchen. Ella slumped against the counter and let out a big breath.

This was ridiculous. Every time she looked at her cell phone, there was another text message from Peter. He wanted to see her. He wanted to talk to her. He wanted to get together JUST 2 TALK.

Ella didn't know what to do.

On the one hand, it made her feel kind of gross that Peter was back in her life, even just in the form of text messages. On the other hand, Ella felt sort of excited that he'd remembered her after a whole year. He still had feelings for her, even though the last time he'd seen her, she'd thrown a Greek salad on him. Maybe she'd meant something to him after all.

It was starting to feel like last summer all over again. Shame and confusion, with that thrill underneath. It made Ella feel like she hadn't reformed at all. That maybe she had just been hanging around, waiting for the next big drama to come along.

But what is so wrong with drama, anyway? Ella thought rebelliously, then sighed again. She shouldn't be so shallow. That was what Kelsi had always called her. Back before guilt and shame had made Ella concentrate on improving her relationship with her sister.

She turned back to the coffeemaker and poured herself a cup. She breathed in the hazelnut aroma that always put her at ease. No, this was not last summer. For all she knew, Peter could be covered in acne, and have gotten a beer belly. Ella cringed at the image of Ugly Peter and decided that she'd turn off her phone and focus on other things, like Jeremy, the lifeguard she had to attract, and Kelsi, the sister she could definitely not betray *again.*

The next evening, Ella knew even without having to locate a mirror that she looked hot in her black halter top and denim miniskirt. She knew that she smelled like Dolce & Gabbana Blue, had minty-fresh breath (thanks to chewing three pieces of Dentyne Ice), and was attracting the attention of several houseboys scattered around the party in the backyard of a Cranberry Lane house.

The moment Beth told her about it, Ella had decided that a lifeguard party was the perfect place for Jeremy to wake up and smell the fabulousness that was Ella Anne Tuttle.

Ella could concede — grudgingly — that maybe there were some guys out there who just didn't go for her. Fine. Not everyone had to love her. It was a big world.

But everybody at least *noticed* her.

Except, apparently, Jeremy.

He hadn't looked her way even once, Ella fumed. Jeremy was standing over in the corner by the pool, completely absorbed in conversation with a bunch of guys. *Completely absorbed.* It took about five minutes for Ella to decide it was time for action.

She sauntered through the party, exchanging a few smiles

and a few more lingering looks, just to keep her spirits up. She headed for Jeremy, and opened her mouth to get his attention.

Which was exactly when Jeremy looked up.

Their eyes met, and Ella felt herself tremble, right down to her knees.

She was so surprised, she tripped and went facedown toward the grass.

Ella only managed to catch herself at the last moment by flinging out an arm and grabbing on to Beth, who happened to be walking by. One shoe buckled beneath her, the fantastic four-inch heel snapping in half. The other flew across the yard and missed impaling Jeremy in the forehead by about one-tenth of a millimeter.

Ella tugged herself upright, ignored the ache in her arm, and had the unpleasant feeling that she was actually blushing. Possibly for the first time in her whole life. Jeremy retrieved the heel and walked it over to Ella, his expression unreadable.

"Wow," he said, and Ella couldn't decide if it was more humiliating that he *wasn't* laughing at her. "You really know how to make an entrance."

Ella wasn't one to accept defeat and personal humiliation, she told herself the next day as she gave herself a pedicure in the bedroom she shared with Kelsi. Especially when she had so little experience with either. So what if she'd been forced to walk home barefoot? So what if Kelsi nearly hurt herself laughing when Ella told her the story in all its gory detail?

She was still laughing, actually, as Ella filed her nails.

Sunlight was streaming in through the windows and it was much too pretty outside to be moody. No matter how much she wanted to be.

"And that was it?" Kelsi was toweling off her hair. "You just tripped and left?"

"Like I was going to stick around after dorking out like that," Ella scoffed. She wiggled her newly painted toes. "Anyway, all I wanted him to do was notice me."

Kelsi pushed her dark hair back from her face. "Mission accomplished," she said with a smirk.

"All attention is good attention," Ella said breezily, trying to convince herself.

Kelsi grinned at her. "Can the famous Ella power be fading? Is that possible?"

"Please." Ella sniffed. "As if."

But as Kelsi left the room, Ella wondered if her sister might be right.

For about twelve seconds.

A few days later, Ella felt enough time had elapsed for Jeremy to have forgotten her little spectacle. She invited herself along to lunch in town with Beth, Adam, and the usual lifeguards, hoping that she could try another attempt at seducing him.

The group was eating at Sammy's, the deli-style lunch place a few doors down from Ahoy. Wasting no time, Ella ordered herself a ham and cheese and sat herself exactly where she wanted to be: next to Jeremy.

As usual, he looked a little nervous when he saw her, but he moved over on the wooden bench so she could fit beside him.

Ella thought he looked adorable in a light blue ribbed T-shirt, board shorts, and flip-flops. Now if only he didn't act like he wasn't sure what planet she came from, she'd consider that a big improvement.

"I haven't been to Sammy's in a long time," Ella spoke softly, almost as if she was telling him a secret. It made him lean a little bit closer, so he could hear her over the din of lunchtime traffic.

"The food here is great," he replied very solemnly. Ella searched his gaze and thought she saw a sparkle of friendliness in there, which perked her up considerably. There was hope after all.

"I can't wait to dig in," she said with a wink, and took a big bite of her sandwich.

"So, Ella," he said, dragging out those three syllables as if he was stalling until he thought of something clever to say. "You left that party before it got good."

"Did you miss me?" she asked, tilting her head to the side.

Jeremy managed to give her a shy smile. "I figured I'd see you again," he said.

"You can see me anytime and anyplace you want to," Ella said in that low voice that usually worked wonders on any breathing male.

Jeremy's smile widened, but he didn't get the eager expression that patented line usually prompted. He didn't even try to grab her thigh, which she'd placed strategically right next to his.

Okay, this guy just might be gay, Ella thought. *Or asexual, like Morrissey.*

"What's your favorite movie?" Jeremy asked abruptly, startling her.

Ella shrugged. "That's a trick question, isn't it? I always think someone's trying to pigeonhole me with a line like that." She flashed him another flirty look. "Like you expect me to say *Legally Blonde* or something cheesy." She took another bite of her sandwich.

Of course, *Legally Blonde* was her favorite movie. But that was beside the point.

"Good answer," Jeremy said with a sheepish grin. "I wasn't expecting that." Then, suddenly, he glanced down at her cleavage, blushed, and looked away.

Ella was finally getting somewhere. She scooted a little bit closer, praying that this was the breakthrough moment.

But then Jeremy looked at his watch instead of at her.

"I have to get back to the beach," he said with a hint of disappointment.

He didn't ask to see her later. He just picked up his plastic tray, got to his feet, and walked away.

Jeremy had Ella way more confused than she wanted to admit. He kept giving her these itty-bitty signals that he was kind of, sort of into her, and each time she tried to capitalize on that, he shuffled away like a scared crab. He *had* scoped out her chest, hadn't he? Ella must have been wearing the most baffled expression when Beth sat down next to her.

"Whoa, what happened to you?" Beth asked, sounding amused.

Ella snapped herself out of her own thoughts. "What do you mean?"

"Maybe you should look in that compact you're always carrying around," Beth said with a mischievous grin.

Ella scrambled to find the mirror in her clutch and immediately opened it up and looked at her face. Everything seemed fine. No food in her teeth.

"Lower," Beth said.

Ella bowed her head. She didn't need a mirror to check out the huge blob of mustard that had fallen down her cleavage and splattered across the top of her left boob.

That was what Jeremy had been looking at while Ella was trying to be all sultry.

This was something that Ella had never expected — she'd suddenly transformed into a complete klutz.

That night, Ella slumped on the couch in front of the TV and tried to find something to watch on cable. Kelsi was out on *another* date, which was beyond depressing.

Her cell phone chirped, and Ella sighed even as she reached for it.

COME ON I WANT 2 C U AT LEAST 1 NCE, Peter wrote. IM SORRY FOR LAST SUMMER U NO THAT, RIGHT?

It made her feel almost dizzy, because it didn't make any sense. And because she had no idea what to think about anything anymore.

With another sigh, Ella shut off the television and wandered into her bedroom. She felt restless.

Maybe she was looking at everything the wrong way. She could still remember what it had felt like to be with Peter. He had made her feel so feverish and delirious. His mouth pressing against hers. His hands skimming over her skin. His fingers digging into her hips. His body on top of hers. She lost her breath for a moment, remembering.

I should just call him, Ella thought then. It wasn't as if she had anything else going on, and following Jeremy around only made her feel like an idiot. She could meet Peter somewhere and no one would ever know about it. Kelsi had Adam now. She might not even care. Everything was different.

Peter had been the first guy Ella had ever pined for, and she'd hated how that made her feel. But now that *he* was doing the pining, Ella found herself very turned on. God, it would be amazing to kiss him again. And touch him . . .

She picked up her phone.

And she put it down again.

First, she would take a shower. Then, Ella would dress herself up in the best outfit she had, and *then,* since it was barely eleven, she would decide what to do. Maybe she would try to talk her way past the bouncers at the Lighthouse. Maybe she'd check out the scene at Ahoy. Maybe she would crash Kelsi's date.

Maybe she would call Peter and see where that led, after all this time.

Maybe.

14

Kelsi knew Adam was going to kiss her. It was their third date and it was time, and what Kelsi found the most surprising was that she was actually looking forward to it. They'd just spent a night at the movies, so she was full of popcorn and good cheer from the cute romantic comedy they'd seen. In fact, she sort of wanted to get the kissing over with, because she had a feeling that the lingering questions she had about the chemistry between them would be solved that easily. And they'd stopped walking in the perfect spot, just out of reach of the nearest streetlight.

She was more than ready.

Adam stepped closer and smiled down at her. Kelsi smiled back. He leaned in and settled his mouth against hers, letting his eyes fall shut. Kelsi kept hers open for a moment, then closed them. His mouth was soft and firm all at once, and she liked the way he held on to her arm with one hand. He kissed her once, then twice, then angled for a third. Kelsi kissed him back. As their tongues touched, she wanted to feel a surge of something exciting and powerful. She wanted to be knocked over, swept away. But really it just felt . . . nice.

When he pulled away, Kelsi didn't know what to say so she smiled again, and tucked her hands into the pockets of her jeans. She felt herself blush and she looked away.

"Let me walk you home," Adam said softly.

Once inside their cottage, Kelsi was relieved to see that her dad was nowhere in sight. Probably in one of the other cottages with the rest of the adults. Sighing slightly, she sank into the couch and tilted her head back to look at the ceiling.

So, kissing Adam had been nice. There was nothing wrong with *nice*. Nice was actually an underrated word. People used it so much that now, if you said something was *nice*, everyone assumed you meant it in a negative way, when maybe that was just the best descriptive adjective.

And really, it was the best word to describe the whole Adam situation. He was *nice*. Their dates were *nice*. It was nice that he walked her home, and nice that he was polite, and nice that he called when he said he would. *Nice* meant a lot, especially when Kelsi was used to boys who could never in a million years be called nice.

Nice was good. She knew that.

But the truth was, nobody wanted to be *nice*. No one wanted their kisses to be *nice*. Everyone wanted fire and passion. Which she didn't feel with Adam. At all.

Her cell phone beeped, and she dug it out of her pocket, surprised to see that the battery was low. She seemed to keep forgetting to charge it when she was in Maine. At home, she was neurotic about charging her phone. Ella was forever having to borrow Kelsi's cell, because Ella, naturally, never remembered to charge her own. But for some reason, once Kelsi hit Maine, she became just as absentminded.

When she clicked into her inbox and saw the name TIM, she felt a rush of excitement shoot through her.

EXCELLENT DRIVING RECORD. PASSION FOR SNACKS. HOW CAN U RESIST?

Kelsi laughed out loud, and then covered her mouth with her hand. She looked around, as if she expected her family to be standing there, witnessing her oddly overexcited reaction to an inanimate object.

All because of one silly text message from one delusional frat boy.

"You are losing it," she told herself, and put Tim out of her mind.

She listened to her voice mail, and heard Jamie's spirited voice singsong a *hello* before her phone shut itself off.

Stupid battery.

Kelsi got up and wandered into her bedroom to find her charger. She heard the shower running in the adjoining bathroom, and Ella's version of singing: tone-deaf and shrill, which was what Kelsi loved about it. She stopped to see if she could figure out what song Ella was mangling, but gave up after Ella sang "baby, baby" off tune several times.

She found her charger on the dresser and plugged her phone in, and then sat on her bed to wait.

Her thoughts immediately went back to Tim. Insane Tim. Insane, funny Tim. Insanely hot, funny Tim. The guys she'd known like Tim in high school — the ones at their brother Catholic school, and the ones she'd run into around town — were pretty much complete losers. Not at all funny, unless you thought *American Pie* was the pinnacle of wit.

It's possible Tim's the exception to the rule, Kelsi thought. Possible, but unlikely. She wished her phone would hurry up and charge, so she could call Jamie back and stop worrying about Tim.

Impatient, Kelsi looked over at Ella's bed and saw that she'd left her cell phone lying there. Why wait for her own phone to charge when Ella's was handy? That was always Ella's rationale when Kelsi found her chatting away on *her* phone at home. Fair was fair.

Kelsi reached over and scooped up Ella's little flip phone, opening it. Apparently, Ella had one new text message. Without thinking, Kelsi hit ENTER.

Idiot, she thought to herself.

And then she realized what she was looking at.

Ella had a long list of incoming text messages. And every one of them was from Peter.

Kelsi felt herself go still. Her head felt fuzzy and somehow no longer connected to her body. She was suddenly focused on the phone in her hand as if nothing else in the world existed.

There are other Peters around, she told herself. But she found herself opening the messages one by one anyway, just to see. To make sure it was some other, unimportant Peter. Some Peter who had never been hers.

One after the other, the messages begged and pleaded and apologized. He wanted to meet up with her. He knew she was in town because he'd seen her. She had to at least talk to him about last summer. Didn't she remember how good it was? And so on.

Kelsi heard a slight sound and realized that it was a whimper, and that it had come from her throat. Which was odd, because she was sure she was screaming.

And just like that, Kelsi knew something that she must have always known. Something she hadn't wanted to know then and didn't want to know now. She remembered it all with such perfect clarity: She'd been sitting there in the pouring rain, waiting for him. The rain had pounded down against the metal of the car, cocooning Kelsi inside the din. Then, finally, he'd appeared, walking through the rain as if he didn't notice it, walking with that particular rolling gait of his that Kelsi had loved. And clinging to his hand was a girl, a girl with blonde hair flattened to her head and her own way of walking — a way of walking Kelsi had decided not to recognize, she now realized. A way of walking she couldn't *let* herself recognize.

Kelsi felt sick to her stomach. Then when she looked up, Ella was standing in the doorway wrapped in a towel and smiling, and Kelsi hated her so much and so intensely that it made her eyes fill with tears.

"Tell me all about your hot date," Ella said cheerfully, rubbing her head with another towel.

"First, why don't you tell me all about Peter," Kelsi said through clenched teeth. "I think I got most of the story from the text messages, but I might be missing a few crucial pieces of information." Her voice sounded terrible, Kelsi thought. Hoarse, like she'd been yelling.

Ella's eyes went wide and then darker, and Kelsi's heart broke completely then, because it was true.

"So fill me in," Kelsi continued. It was like she couldn't stop herself. "Maybe you can show me how it works. How you decide to hook up with your sister's boyfriend."

"You don't understand," Ella began, and she sounded different, too, like someone else. Someone younger, less sure of herself. Someone shaky and panicked.

"Then explain it to me," Kelsi suggested, her voice beyond harsh this time. She was so angry and hurt that she thought her body might shut down completely. "Explain to me how my younger sister screwed my boyfriend fifteen minutes after we broke up."

Ella flinched and then her eyes filled with tears. Kelsi felt queasy, because she hadn't really thought about that part — what Ella had actually done with Peter. She'd just thrown that out there to hurt Ella. But now she knew.

"You had sex with him?" she asked, and hated herself for sounding so hurt. She wished she could sound strong. Righteously indignant. But Kelsi's voice was doing just as it pleased.

"I . . ." The tears began to roll down Ella's cheeks. "I never would have done anything with him — I totally gave up when I saw how into him you were, but then there was this one night in the car and *he* was the one who started it, I swear —"

"You're pathetic," Kelsi spat at her, but she had to whisper because she was afraid she was going to start sobbing. "You hated the fact that he chose me, didn't you? You couldn't stand it. You had to be the pretty one, the popular one, the one all the boys wanted. You couldn't believe someone could like me instead of you." Kelsi understood; she was supposed to be in the shadows while Ella stood in the spotlight. It had been that way their whole lives.

"It wasn't like that!" Ella sobbed. Her face was twisted, and she looked almost ugly. Kelsi felt like she was seeing her sister for the first time. "I'm so sorry, Kelsi. I never meant to hurt you," Ella added.

"So you were nice to me afterward, what? To make up for it?" Kelsi wiped angrily at her face, where the tears had started to stain. "It was all just part of this? What you did?"

"No!" Ella's eyes searched the room wildly, and then came back to focus on Kelsi. "I just wished I could take it back!"

"You're not my sister anymore." Kelsi could hear the cold anger in her voice. It was making her shake. "You betrayed me. You lied to me. You're a selfish, vapid little bitch. Stay the hell away from me."

She took the phone and threw it, making Ella jump, although it went nowhere near her. Ella was clutching her towel with one hand, and she gave a small whimper when the phone case broke open as it hit the wall and spilled to the floor.

"Kelsi . . ." she said, pleading. Kelsi hadn't seen Ella cry in years, not since she was a very little girl. Like then, it made her whole body weaken in a flash of sympathy, and Kelsi hated the part of her that cared.

"I hope you and that asshole are very happy together," Kelsi snarled at her. "You're perfect for each other!"

She tore through the house and ran out the back door. She found herself in the backyard, alone in the dark.

She sank to her knees in the grass and looked up at the night sky, as if she might find some answers written in the constellations. There were so many stars, and they were all too bright. They crowded the sky and made everything blurry.

Or maybe that's because of the tears.

Beth sprawled across her bed, with her feet propped up against the headboard.

"So how's Adam?" George was asking.

"Okay, I guess," Beth said, trying to sound careless. Why shouldn't she *feel* careless? Nothing had happened, or would *ever* happen with Adam. Yes, Beth liked the fact that a hot guy possibly liked *her* — she wasn't the sort of girl hot guys noticed, usually — but it was all harmless, right?

"He's actually out on a date with Kelsi as we speak," Beth added, as if she had to prove something.

George let out an exaggerated sigh and countered with, "Great. So why are you being cagey and weird?"

"Way to turn that around on me, Mr. Too-Tired-to-Call-Last-Night," Beth retorted, trying to steer the topic away from Adam.

She wondered how could she be in love with George and

so irritated by him at the same time. But how could she *not* be in love with George? She'd loved him for longer than she'd even known she loved him. They'd been friends for years before they ever hooked up. But the minute she was without him, Beth was finding herself all worked up about someone else. Someone who didn't know her that well, a guy who didn't have a history with her, still found her to be attractive and fun. And who made her feel . . . wonderful.

As opposed to this conversation, which was making her feel like shit.

"I'm not turning anything around, Miss Never-Answers-Her-Phone," George shot back. "And last night was the first time in the entire history of the world that I didn't call you fifty-seven times. You could try answering one call, just for fun."

"What are you talking about?" Beth groaned, trying not to get worried.

"Yeah, well, maybe I'm saying you'd rather be talking with this Adam guy instead of me," George said, continuing the same half joking, half fighting they seemed to have every time they talked. "Maybe this guy deliberately saves the good-looking girls so he can work the whole hero thing on them."

"Oh my God, you're driving me insane!" Beth cried, faking indignation.

"Just as long as I'm still making an impression," George said swiftly. And as usual, Beth could tell that underneath the jokey tone, he was trying to make a point.

Stay the hell away from Adam.

"Trust me, you make the *only* impression," she assured him.

"That's much better," George said sincerely. "More of that stuff, please."

"I can't believe you're getting so crazy about some guy," Beth told him.

Not that Adam was just *some guy*, Beth told herself crossly. It was all so much more complicated than that. She swallowed hard. Maybe she should break up with George, just for a little while, until she figured things out with Adam. Beth had never understood her friends back home who two-timed their boyfriends and ended up sobbing in the school bathroom. If you weren't sure how you felt about someone anymore, you should break up. It was simple.

Except it didn't feel simple. The thought of breaking up with George made her feel winded, as if she'd been knocked down.

Beth rolled over. Now it was the end of July and she felt the entire summer had been twisted inside out. She felt like crying, except that in reality she had nothing to cry about. Nothing bad was really happening, except for what was going on in her head, where nobody else could see it.

"I'm crazy about *you*," George said. "I can't say it enough."

Despite herself, Beth laughed. "Say it one more time."

"I'm crazy about you, Bethy. I'm counting down the seconds until I can see you again."

"I can't wait to see you, too," she told him.

Because right in that moment, she meant it with all her heart.

*   *   *

After getting off the phone with George, Beth was having another internal debate — this time, trying to choose between the DVDs of *Mean Girls* and *10 Things I Hate About You* — when Kelsi burst into the cottage, crying hysterically. Beth sprang to her feet, terrified. She'd never seen her cousin like this. Something seriously horrible must have happened.

"Ella" was all that Kelsi managed to say.

"What happened to her?" Beth asked. She grabbed her cousin, steering her toward the couch and steeling herself for the worst. "You have to tell me what's going on!" she ordered.

"Ella," Kelsi got out, between gulps for air, "slept with Peter." Beth sucked in a breath, thinking she couldn't have heard that right. "Last summer," Kelsi said over another sob, "she slept with Peter."

Kelsi dissolved into a fresh batch of tears. She hid her face behind her hands and cried.

Beth held on tightly and swore she wouldn't let go until Kelsi wanted her to.

"This is definitely a Ben & Jerry's situation," Beth said a while later, digging two pints out of the freezer. Misery demanded double-fisting with New York Super Chunk and Oatmeal Cookie Chunk. Chunks were for times of crisis.

She handed Kelsi one of the pints and a big spoon, and climbed onto the bed with her own pint to sit cross-legged beside her cousin.

Kelsi had cried for two solid hours, and was now

115

swollen-eyed, but calm. She'd put on a pair of Beth's black sweats with white piping down the legs and a hooded sweatshirt. Beth didn't think she'd ever seen Kelsi so upset.

They both dug in to their respective pints, and were quiet for a moment of appreciation. When Kelsi gave a sad sigh, Beth knew the divine taste of the ice cream could only work so much magic.

"I don't think I can look at her again," Kelsi said sadly. "I guess it's a good thing I'm going off to college."

"There's no way that this is a misunderstanding?" Beth was hopeful. Just because nothing was ever that simple in real life didn't mean it *couldn't* be.

"No." Kelsi sounded certain.

"I can't believe she would do something like that," Beth said, frowning into her ice cream.

"Oh, come on." Kelsi's voice crackled with bitterness. "Of course she would do something like that. Ella thinks every guy on the planet is just waiting for a chance with her. She thinks she can treat anybody however she wants and they'll just, like, suck it up for the opportunity to be near her."

"I don't know if that's true," Beth murmured. She didn't know how to talk about this. She didn't feel like she could fully participate in Ella-bashing, and yet — sleeping with Kelsi's boyfriend? It was pretty heinous.

An unwelcome thought took root then. Imagine if this was a different situation, Beth realized. If Beth had actually acted on her growing feelings for Adam, what would that do to George if he found out? She pictured him sitting across from her with that same hollow, hurt look in his eyes that Kelsi was displaying, and she shuddered.

"Ella is selfish," Kelsi snapped. "She's conceited, shallow, and apparently a complete ho. I don't know why I thought she was even *capable* of changing."

"Okay," Beth said a little cautiously. "I think what she did is really shitty. But, you know, it's not like she did it all alone."

"Peter was always an asshole," Kelsi said. "Now I see that he's the kind of asshole who cheats on me with my sister, and then likes it so much he's still chasing her a year later." She let out a bleak laugh. "Maybe that means *I'm* the asshole."

"You are not," Beth said firmly. "You can't blame yourself for what they did, Kelsi."

"She's my *sister*," Kelsi whispered. Her eyes were huge and weepy. "She betrayed me. How could she?"

"I don't know," Beth whispered back. "I don't understand it at all."

But the worst part was, there was something Beth was very afraid to acknowledge. Suddenly, she could understand betrayal all too well.

Much later, when Kelsi had curled herself up into a ball and was passed out beside her, Beth lay wide awake, thinking.

She could never do what Ella had done. Family was family, and that should come first. Beth felt pretty strongly about that.

But that was so easy to say when you *weren't* tempted. When George was so far away and Adam was so close, it almost seemed to make sense that Beth should cross that line.

It felt so good to be wanted. To catch all those intense stares and understand what they meant and that they were all just for her.

Stop it! a little voice screamed inside Beth's head. She burrowed her face fiercely into her pillow. She could only imagine how wounded George would be — Kelsi was this upset, and she'd only dated Peter a month or so. Cheating on George would kill him. And no matter how messed up she felt about George these days, Beth didn't think she could survive knowing she'd hurt him.

Her eyes never closed that night.

16

Ella had thought, for almost a year now, that the worst thing that could possibly happen would be Kelsi finding out what had happened with Peter. But it turned out that Kelsi's *finding out* wasn't half as bad as what happened next: Kelsi hating her.

That part of it was almost funny, actually. Ella had spent years being irritated to death by Kelsi. It seemed ridiculous — in a way that tore at her heart — to suddenly regret losing someone she'd only valued for so short a time. Ella was surprised how much it hurt. Seriously hurt, like some kind of emotional flu that made all her bones ache with it. Even if there was a tiny part of her that was relieved that all the secrecy was over now — Kelsi knew and there was no more worrying *when* or *if*.

The morning after the Peter disaster, Ella wandered out into the yard to find Beth already there with the three younger cousins, refereeing a game of badminton. Jessi whaled on the birdie, and it went completely wide of the net, which sent both her brothers into gales of laughter. Her next birdie nearly took Jordan's head off. *A girl after my own heart,* Ella thought. Then she saw the way Beth pinched her lips together when she caught sight of Ella approaching, and Ella's stomach sank. Kelsi must have told her.

"Are you going down to the beach?" Ella asked in a casual tone. If Beth was mad at her, too, there was nothing she could do except muddle through it.

"Later," Beth said. Ella thought that Beth was concentrating a little too hard on the badminton. *She doesn't want to look at me,* Ella realized. She felt that much worse, and then, defiantly, sort of mad about it. Why was Beth taking sides?

"Well," Ella said, feeling awkward and angry. "I don't think —"

"Look," Beth said, cutting her off. Ella didn't like the expression on her cousin's face. It was hard and hot and made Ella feel like crying again. "I was up all night with Kelsi so I'm a little wiped, okay?"

"You don't even know my side of it all," Ella said, her voice cracking.

"Is there one?" Beth asked, her eyebrows raised. "I don't know, El. This situation seems like a no-brainer to me."

Ella didn't have a response. She felt like her heart had gone through a food processor. The guilt was that overwhelming.

"I just . . ." Ella couldn't finish the sentence. In her head, she had so many different explanations — and maybe that was the problem. They all tangled around each other and by the time they got to her mouth, they hardly made sense anymore.

"I don't want to talk about this right now," Beth said, and turned her head away. "It's not my business anyway."

Dismissed, Ella thought, and told herself her eyes were just tired, not tearing up again. She was sick of crying over milk she'd spilled herself.

A few days later, Ella found herself wandering through the little shops in town, comparing the prices of driftwood art and seashell necklaces. She picked up a statuette of a clamshell, complete with googly eyes and felt ears, and managed not to make a face. Did people really buy this junk? She put the clamshell back on its shelf, and smiled politely at the woman behind the counter.

Stepping out into the afternoon sunshine, Ella settled her sunglasses back on her nose. Kelsi was still avoiding her like the plague, while Beth was all wrapped up in G-2. But Ella was cool with it. She didn't mind being alone, she told herself. It was nice not to check with anyone else if she wanted to hang out on the pier at night, staring at the water and ignoring the millions of kissing couples. It was all Ella, all the time, and why shouldn't she enjoy her own company?

She set off down the sidewalk, avoiding a gridlock of strollers. *Who am I kidding?* She was lonely — a new feeling for her. And she was beginning to worry that maybe she didn't even know what love was. It sounded melodramatic when she thought about it like that, but deep down, it rang true. She'd messed up pretty badly when it came to loving her sister, so maybe it wasn't a surprise that she couldn't seem to find a real, loving relationship with a boy. Every time she started to focus on a guy, she got distracted by some other hot body or chiseled face, and Ella forgot all about the promises she made to herself. Maybe some people weren't made to have real relationships. Maybe some people were supposed to be on their own.

Ella tried to convince herself that she didn't mind if she was one of those people. She just wished that if that were true, it didn't make her feel so empty and scared.

And that, Ella decided as she headed toward the nail salon, was about all the self-pity she could stomach. She was going to treat herself to a pedicure, and then she was going to move on. One way or another.

Evening was just starting to stretch out across the sky as Ella headed home. She opted for the long way around, so she could saunter past the lifeguard station and see if a certain frustrating-but-adorable boy happened to be hanging around.

Bingo. Jeremy was there, locking up the station and pocketing the keys. He'd pulled on a oversize charcoal gray sweatshirt, and looked deliciously windblown.

Ella quickly checked herself for potential humiliations. No food to dribble, and nothing to trip over. She was wearing flip-flops. She was about as safe as she was going to be.

She hung back as Jeremy swung a JanSport bag over his shoulder, and let him turn around and notice her.

When his mouth curved into a shy smile, Ella felt something warm pass over her body, and she was sure it wasn't the breeze.

"Hey," she said.

"Hi," he replied. He walked closer to her. Ella had to tilt her head back to keep looking him in the eye, and there was something exhilarating about having to do that.

"Are you okay?" he asked, startling her. Ella nodded, suddenly feeling choked up by his kindness. Nobody had been nice to her in days.

"Um," Jeremy said softly. "Can I walk you home?" A red flush started behind his ears, Ella noticed, but he didn't look away.

Ella didn't feel as amused or triumphant as she did when other guys finally succumbed to her devices. And besides, Jeremy wasn't really falling for her tricks. He was warming up to her because he wanted to, which made her happy. And, after her fight with Kelsi, she hadn't thought happiness would be possible again. She swallowed the lump in her throat.

"That would be great," she whispered, and smiled a real smile for the first time in what seemed like eternity.

17

Over the next few days, Kelsi avoided the cottage as much as possible, and slept on the couch whenever she wasn't crashing at Beth's. Her dad noticed that something was up with her and Ella, but he hadn't pried, which was for the best. Kelsi didn't feel like talking to anyone. She decided that she would spend the rest of her days in Pebble Beach exploring the great outdoors, communing with nature the way she used to do when she was that trusting, idiot hippie chick.

The worst part of it, Kelsi thought one morning while she was getting tea at the organic café in town, was that she had no real reason to be upset. She hadn't learned anything new, had she? Peter was an asshole and Ella . . . It hurt just to think about Ella, but Kelsi knew that her little sister had always been exactly what she was now revealed to be: egocentric, careless, recklessly cruel. It had just been the past year — when Ella was all sweetness and light — that had been out of character, not what she'd done last summer.

By that rationale, I shouldn't be depressed at all, Kelsi thought, dunking her tea bag in hot water with unnecessary force. She should have known better. She propped her chin in her hand and stared across the café's outside seating area, her eyes not focusing on anything.

Her phone vibrated in the pocket of her overalls, which startled her. She jumped a little bit, and then pulled it out.

Tim.

At first, she wasn't at all sure she wanted to talk to him. But then it dawned on her that Tim was totally unrelated to anything else that was going on in her life. He didn't even know Ella existed, which made him just about the only person Kelsi could imagine talking to at the moment.

"I can't believe you picked up," Tim said when she answered.

"Neither can I," Kelsi said, sitting back in her chair.

"I thought it would take at least six calls."

"Six?" Kelsi wrinkled up her nose as she processed that. "Why six? Why not seven? Or, like, two?"

"Something about you, that night at the bonfire . . ." There was a teasing lilt to his voice. "Told me you were a six-calls kind of girl."

"You're completely bullshitting me."

"Possibly," Tim agreed.

"I guess I should be impressed that you admit it," Kelsi said.

"You should definitely be impressed by me," Tim told her. "I keep trying to make that clear."

"That's why you called?" Kelsi realized she was smiling. "To impress me?"

"I called because you look cute in your overalls," Tim said.

Kelsi sat up straight and looked around, her heart pounding. He wasn't sitting anywhere near her, which meant he had to be somewhere on the street, or even —

"Boo," he said, walking out from inside the café and snapping his phone shut. "You looked much cuter a few seconds ago, when you were smiling. Just so you know."

"You mean before I knew you were stalking me?" Kelsi glared at him as she turned off her phone.

"I don't think my desire for morning coffee makes me a stalker, Kelsi," Tim said in that carefree way of his. "How was I supposed to know you'd be here? Pebble Beach is a small town. There are only so many places to hide."

She continued to glare at him, which had no discernible effect.

"So anyway," he said after a moment. "Want to hang out? You look like you could use some fun."

"Describe what you consider *fun*," Kelsi shot back.

Tim's grin widened.

"Hmm. I don't think we're ready for that yet," he said. "That's a third-date kind of thing, definitely."

"Which will never happen," Kelsi told him immediately. "Because we're not dating." *As if,* she thought, actually snorting to herself. Like she would be dumb enough to date this guy.

"Relax, doll face." Tim seemed unfazed. "But if we *were* dating, I would wait until the third date to bring out the big guns. That's all I'm saying."

"I'm totally opposed to guns," Kelsi said in her deeply offended, liberal hippie voice. That's what Ella always called it — not that she wanted to think about Ella. "So maybe you should keep them to yourself."

"You're a smart girl," Tim said. If he noticed the deeply offended liberal hippie voice, or the cold, anti-Ella voice, he didn't show it. "You're supposed to be wowed when I bust out my metaphors."

Kelsi rolled her eyes, but maddeningly, she couldn't keep herself from smiling.

"I have an idea," Tim said after a moment. "But you have to trust me."

"Count me out," Kelsi said through a laugh that slipped out of her mouth when she wasn't thinking.

"You *have* to trust me," he said again, smiling a little.

"Well," Kelsi said, "I'll try."

Tim laughed. "I guess that's as good as it gets," he said. "Come on. The day is slipping away."

He put his hand on her wrist and tugged her to her feet like he didn't have the slightest doubt that she'd be thrilled if he dragged her off somewhere.

As for Kelsi, she was surprised to notice that when she stopped trying to push Tim away, she actually kind of liked having him close by.

18

Beth had tried everything — sensory deprivation, reverse psychology, excessive exercising, anything to get her to stop thinking about Adam *that way*. But none of it worked. She was so exhausted from it that she just wanted to raise a white flag and admit defeat. Beth looked over at Adam one afternoon and the little voice sounded in her head, saying, *Just surrender.*

"What's wrong?" he asked. He'd turned his head quicker than she'd thought he might, and caught her gawking at him.

"Nothing's wrong!" Beth said abruptly. She smiled, embarrassed, and hoped the heat she could feel creeping along her jaw didn't actually show.

They were spending another one of Adam's lunch hours sitting up on their favorite rock overlooking the beach. Beth let her feet drum against the stone beneath her. She wished everything could be as simple as when she was staring blankly out at the sea of water that stretched all the way to the horizon and then beyond.

"I've called Kelsi a couple of times, but I haven't heard back," Adam said. "Did she go on that road trip already?"

That pulsing in my heart means nothing, Beth told herself.

"Not yet," she replied nonchalantly. "I was supposed to go with them, but it turns out I can't."

Because George is supposed to come that weekend, she thought. *My fabulous boyfriend, George.*

Adam looked at her for a moment, but didn't say anything.

The silence loomed over them for a while, and Beth did everything she could not to stare at Adam. She was hyper-aware of him beside her. His skin was still damp despite the streaming sunshine. He smelled like a heady mix of coconut suntan lotion and salt water. She knew that if she smiled at him, he would smile back and his eyes would light up in a way that never failed to turn her to mush. But there was nothing wrong with yearning, was there? It was action that got you into trouble.

"I really like Kelsi," Adam said suddenly, putting his sandwich down and brushing the crumbs from his hands. The queasy, jealous feeling Beth was becoming familiar with snaked around her abdomen and pulled tight.

"Kelsi's great," Beth said staunchly. She had no right to say anything else. She had no right to feel that sharp pang.

"You Tuttle ladies are all very cool," Adam was saying. He turned his head and their eyes met. Beth found she was holding her breath.

"It's like a family thing," she managed to say, hoping that didn't sound as stupid as she thought it did.

"Here's the real thing," Adam said, ignoring her attempt at humor. He was still looking at Beth in that intense way.

And she knew, somehow, that she had to make sure he didn't say whatever he was about to say. But she didn't do anything that might distract him. In fact, Beth did the exact opposite.

"Here's what thing?" she asked, and she could hear how breathy she sounded. *This is terrible,* she thought. *You have to stop this.*

But Beth was frozen there on the rock with sand between her toes, her hair blowing slightly in the wind. And the only thing she saw was the expression on Adam's face.

"I like your cousin," he said, his eyes fixed on hers. "But you know who I *really* like?"

Beth knew this was where she should end this conversation. But he was smiling, and she could feel herself willing this into reality.

"Who?" she asked breathlessly.

"You."

Oh, God.

"Of course you, Beth," he added, after a moment of silence. "It's probably pretty obvious by now how I feel about you."

There was no taking that back, Beth thought in the endless moment they were transfixed by each other. Of course she knew. She'd known each time they accidentally touched hands or knees while they were surfing. She'd known when he'd made those throwaway comments about skinny-dipping and when he'd tensed up at the mention of George. And she'd secretly delighted in that knowledge. But knowing it was so different from hearing Adam say it.

Everything was all too real now.

"Adam . . ." Suddenly, there was a lump in her throat. She glanced away. "I have a boyfriend."

"I know you do," he said immediately. "I didn't intend for this to happen. But I can't get you out of my head, Beth."

She waited for him to say something else, but he didn't. Beth couldn't take simmering in the sun with these feelings swirling all around them.

"Maybe I should go," she said, sliding off the rock. He jumped down, too, and there was an awkward instant where Beth should have taken off, but instead felt stuck there in the sand.

"I don't mean to make things hard for you," Adam said.

Beth looked up at him, and saw all the confusion she felt written across his face.

"I just . . ." She shook her head. "I just have to go, okay?"

"I think this —" Adam never took his eyes off her face. "What's happening between us is special."

He moved closer as he said it. Beth looked up at him, and swallowed hard. He was so close now. She felt fear race through her — and something else. Longing. Desire.

"Adam, no." But it was like she barely spoke at all. Like she'd only meant to speak her words and they had gotten lost somewhere between her head and her voice.

He didn't say anything else, just leaned in and kissed her.

Beth felt his lips against hers, soft, sweet, and warm, and so new they made her tremble. Then his arms went around her. His mouth was urgent, hungry, eager to consume her. She responded to his kiss, drinking him in, her fingers in his hair.

Then she pulled away, breathless. She shook her head, overcome by what they'd done.

"Please, don't fight this," Adam whispered.

And for a split second, Beth agreed with every single particle of her being.

So it felt almost heroic when she forced herself to turn and walk away.

19

"You're bringing me here for some sort of weird sex thing, aren't you?" Kelsi asked, pulling her wrist out of Tim's grip.

He'd talked her into going on a nature walk so that they could check out these unusual boulders on the outskirts of town. They'd been strolling through grass, wildflowers, blueberry patches, and ungainly rocks for the last twenty minutes.

And now they'd stopped in a spot so secluded that if Kelsi had fallen like that proverbial tree in the woods, no one would hear her scream.

Tim gave her a sideways glance and a smirk. "Please, Kelsi. You wish."

She spotted a NO TRESPASSING sign that had a picture of a large dog biting off some poor guy's arm and was suddenly terrified. "Holy shit, we're going to die."

"Do you want the good news or the bad news?" Tim

asked, crossing his arms over his chest and eyeing her the same way she'd been eyeing the sign.

"Both."

"Fine. The bad news is, yes, we're going to die. That's what happens when you're not immortal. But the good news is, we probably won't die today."

"That's so comforting," Kelsi said, rolling her eyes.

"Watch out for the rocks," Tim warned as they started off again. "Sometimes they move when you least expect it."

"It's so cool," Kelsi observed. "The boulders were dropped here so long ago. Like footprints or something. They've been here forever." Longer than anyone she knew had been alive. Longer than Pebble Beach had even existed. So long ago, in fact, that the things people did just a year before suddenly seemed trivial.

Tim's smile now seemed warmer and less smirky. "My theory is that a glacier covered all of this. It would explain why it's still so cold most of the year."

He led her down a path that seemed to be a figment of his imagination. It zigged and zagged its way down the rock-strewn cliff, and abruptly led them into a perfect, private cove. It was absolutely breathtaking.

"This is beautiful," Kelsi said in a near whisper.

"It's a secret," Tim said. His eyes were bright when he took off his shades and looked at her. "You can't ever bring anyone else here. There's a pirate curse. Maybe more than one."

"Like I could ever find that path again!"

"Pirate curse," he warned her a second time. "You saw what happened in *Pirates of the Caribbean,* didn't you?"

"I saw Johnny Depp," Kelsi retorted.

"Trust me," he said with that likable, arrogant tone of his. "I'm way more fun than him."

Not that she was counting, but Kelsi had completely lost track of how many times she'd laughed that day.

It turned out that Tim knew all kinds of secret places in and around Pebble Beach. Kelsi had spent every summer she could remember there, and she'd never even heard of the secret cove. Much less the equally hidden inlet he took her to the following afternoon — complete with a picnic lunch he claimed he'd packed for himself anyway so he might as well share it with her. The day after that, Tim rowed them out in a dinghy to one of the tiny, rocky islands that dotted the coastline. The island he chose was hardly more than a large sandbar, with rocks and a few trees.

"How do you know all these places?" Kelsi inquired. "Are you a tour guide or something?"

"Can't I just have an interest in something besides *you?* " Tim asked, pretending to be offended. "Maybe I appreciate nature."

"Uh, you're a frat boy," Kelsi said. "Doesn't your world revolve around beer and football?"

"Prejudice is so unattractive," Tim chided her. "I should make you swim back."

"You wouldn't dare."

"Oh, I would definitely dare," Tim corrected her. "But I won't."

He led her up to the highest point of the tiny island, where they sat and looked at the cluster of the town back across the bay. The pier jutted out into the water, and people milled around on the stretch of sand to each side. Behind them, the quaint little buildings lined the main streets and the evergreens framed everything. The whole scene looked like a perfect picture postcard of a Maine summer town. Like Pebble Beach was a place where nothing bad ever happened and no one ever got hurt.

Kelsi must have made a slight sound, because when Tim looked at her, his face was without any trace of its usual smirk.

"What's wrong?" he asked.

Maybe she just needed to talk to someone. Maybe she was unprepared for the obvious concern in his gaze. Maybe she'd been lulled into believing that a guy like Tim really *could* be sensitive. Kelsi didn't know. But she took a big breath, and then everything spilled out. Ella, Peter, last summer, the fight — everything.

"Wow," Tim murmured a long while later. He was sitting propped up against the nearest tree. "That's some serious stuff. I'm sorry you had to go through that."

"I don't even know what I feel about any of it," Kelsi said, her shoulders hunching forward.

"Except shitty."

"Except that," Kelsi agreed.

They sat there another moment or so, and Kelsi suddenly wished she hadn't said anything. He knew now. He knew what a total loser she was. He knew that her little sister was so devious that she could steal boyfriends from her. There was nothing about the situation that wasn't humiliating.

"Your ex-boyfriend sounds like an ass," Tim said matter-of-factly. "I don't know what your sister was thinking, either."

"Ella's never been big on thinking about anything other than herself," Kelsi said bitterly. "That's why I can't ever speak to her again."

"You need a plan," Tim said.

"To do what? Murder her?" Kelsi smirked. "I have several."

"Easy, Terminator," he said. "I mean a plan to deal with all this. You can't avoid your sister for the rest of your life."

"No, but I *can* avoid her for the rest of the summer," Kelsi said. "After that, I'll be in college."

"That's one way to play it," Tim said thoughtfully. "Except eventually you'll have to deal with her, so why not do it sooner rather than later?"

"What do you mean?"

"I mean, you figure out how to deal with her so it's on *your* terms. Why should you hide from her? You didn't do anything wrong." Tim flipped a twig between his fingers. "She's the one who should be ashamed." He said it very deliberately, like he wanted Kelsi to hear that part the most. She felt her face heat up again.

"You don't know Ella," she said wryly.

There was a breeze blowing, and the sound of the water lapping against the shore was almost hypnotic. Kelsi let it lull her into calmness for a moment, and then groaned as a new thought hit her. She *would* have to deal with Ella sooner than she thought. *The road trip.*

"Oh no," she said. "I totally spaced on our trip to Amherst. I can't do it. That's a recipe for disaster."

"Not if you bring me along," Tim said, smiling slightly.

"Forget it," Kelsi said. "I'm gonna e-mail my cousin today and tell her it's not happening."

"Think about it this way," Tim suggested. "I come along and act as a buffer between you and your sister. You get to see your cousin at Amherst, I get to U Mass orientation. Everyone wins."

Kelsi stared at him and blinked a few times.

"You want to be my buffer, huh? Why?" she asked him.

"It's simple. You need me and I need you," he replied.

Kelsi got the odd sense that it *wasn't* as simple as that. But, in that moment, she was grateful for how Tim had phrased it.

"I don't know," she said. "I'm not sure I can bear to talk to Ella long enough to tell her I still want to go."

"Sure you can," Tim said, with a self-assured smile. "And then I'll deal with her. It'll be great. *I'll* be great. I promise."

Kelsi frowned.

"Listen," Tim said, leaning forward and taking her hands between his. "You have to show her that even though what she did sucks, you're okay."

"I'm not sure I *am* okay," Kelsi whispered.

"But you will be."

Maybe it was all the sunshine, or the sea air, but she believed him.

And maybe it was crazy, but she was starting to realize that she liked Tim. She liked him a lot.

Late that night, and Kelsi woke up when she heard Ella creep into the room they shared. She heard the click of Ella's bedside lamp and the creak of the floorboards. She cracked her eyes open just enough to watch her sister shrug out of her clothes and kick them out of her way. God only knew what Ella had been out doing. *Or, more likely, who,* Kelsi thought with a smirk.

Watching Ella made Kelsi feel unexpectedly sad. There was something so defeated and still sort of brave about the way she carried herself. It made Kelsi want to comfort her — and *that* made Kelsi so mad she wanted to kick something.

"We're leaving for Amherst early Thursday morning," Kelsi spoke, enjoying the way Ella jumped at the sound of her voice.

"Um," Ella said, and coughed a little bit. "Uh, yeah . . . Okay."

"A friend of mine is coming," Kelsi continued. "I want to leave exactly at nine thirty. Not whenever you feel like getting up."

"Sure, right. Whatever you want," Ella said quietly. She

looked very young then, her eyes big and fixed on Kelsi as if she thought Kelsi might leap up and attack her. Kelsi refused to feel even a drop of sympathy.

"And I don't want to talk about any of this while we're there," Kelsi said. She rolled over so she faced Ella fully. "Jamie doesn't need to know, so let's just pretend nothing happened. Do you think you can do that?"

Ella looked as if she might say something, but she just swallowed and nodded, picking at her gingham bedspread with one hand.

"Yes," she said softly.

"Good," Kelsi snapped, and pulled her comforter over her head.

She heard Ella take a few deep breaths, and then it was silent for a while. And then, much later, she heard Ella climb into bed and settle down for the night, shutting off the light so the room was filled with darkness and the far-off gleam of moon and stars.

Kelsi imagined that she and her sister were separated by much more than the space between their single beds as they lay wide awake in the darkness for hours.

It wasn't as if Adam did anything deliberately. Neither did Beth. She showed up at her usual time on Wednesday, and when he came down the beach for his break, neither one of them mentioned what had happened. It was like everything was still wonderfully platonic. As if they both hadn't felt the wild heat of their kiss.

But it seemed like their hands bumped together more often that day. Their boards seemed to crash together more regularly than usual, and Adam had to steady both of them, which also required touching. Every time she felt his skin against hers, Beth had the same thought: *I should tell him to stop*. But then she thought that mentioning their touching would draw attention to the fact that she was *noticing* it in the first place.

So she said nothing.

That afternoon when she said good-bye to Adam, Beth

noticed that they both seemed to linger in the grass by the edge of the dunes. Adam looked as if he was thinking of something else to say while she kept forcing a smile.

"So," he said finally. "Feel like dinner tonight?"

They'd been having dinner together practically all summer. Now, of course, it meant something different. But Beth couldn't bear to say no.

"Okay," she said. "As friends."

"Friends," he echoed.

She could feel him watching her as she walked away.

"I'm not sure what the deal is," George said on the phone that evening. "There's a slight chance that I might have to sub for this other guy, but if that happens, I'm definitely coming up *next* weekend. Oh, and I asked for time off, so we can spend most of the week together when I do make it up there."

"Okay," Beth said. It was one of those "okays" that came out sounding more like "that sucks." Such a pissy girlfriend noise. Normally, it would have made both of them laugh.

George sighed. "What?"

"It's just that I was supposed to go to Amherst this weekend," Beth reminded him. "Kelsi and Ella are leaving tomorrow morning. But I canceled because you were coming. . . ." Everything about her tone was weird and wrong, she thought, but she couldn't seem to help herself.

"As far as I know, I still am." George's patience sounded like it was waning. "I'm just saying that *maybe* something might come up."

"Fine."

"Okay."

"Great," Beth snapped. And then there was another silence, which Beth broke by sighing. "I should go," she said at last, failing to mention that she'd be meeting Adam for dinner.

"I can't wait to see you," George said, his voice cajoling, perhaps in hopes that she might soften a little bit. "It's been so long."

"I know," Beth said, and she felt herself soften, despite herself. "I think I've forgotten what you look like."

"Don't worry," George said, and Beth could hear the smile in his voice. "I'll remind you."

This is fine, Beth thought as she and Adam walked side by side down Peachtree Road. Nothing too awkward. So what if they hadn't said more than two words to each other over a painfully tense dinner at Ahoy?

Beth didn't know if she felt miserable or nervous. Maybe it was the same thing.

"You know what?" Adam said abruptly. He came to a dead stop. "I think maybe I should go home."

"Um, okay," Beth was confused, and also, stupidly, hurt. She didn't want to stop being with him so soon, even if things were so weird.

"I just can't pretend this isn't awkward," Adam said. "It's easier for you, obviously."

Easy? The word echoed in Beth's head as anger surged through her. Was he kidding?

"You don't know anything about what it's like for me," she snapped at him.

Beth's emotions were traveling at light speed, and she knew that even if she pulled the emergency brake, nothing would change what was happening. She wheeled around, determined to get as far away from him as possible, as quickly as possible. She charged up the street, her long legs eating up the distance, but she could hear that he was right behind her.

"Look," he said a few minutes later, following her to the dirt road that forked back toward the cottages. "I'm sorry. What do you want me to say?"

"I . . . want things to go back the way they were!" Beth cried, whirling around. "Back at the beginning of the summer. I just want to hang out and laugh and have fun without all this . . ." She didn't know what to call it. "You know!"

"I don't know how to do that," Adam said softly, his eyes intent on her face. "Beth . . ." His voice trailed away, ending almost in a question. He took a step closer to her.

On the dirt road, the trees cocooned them in darkness. In the shadows, Beth felt as if Adam could see right through her, into her soul.

He reached out with one hand and wrapped it gently around her shoulder. She felt the heat of his palm soak into her skin and travel along her body.

She meant to say something — anything — but then he was so close, and she trailed her hands along his chest and tilted her head back so she could look up into his face.

He whispered her name.

Then he leaned down and kissed her, and Beth's whirling thoughts came to a rest. He tasted a little bit like mint and his lips were so warm. She didn't even think to pull back this time.

They kissed again, and again. Like they'd been saving up all summer, and were pouring all those days of longing into each new touch of their mouths and tongues. This was what she'd been wanting for so very long. Beth ran her hands along his shoulders, and down his strong arms, and then around his waist, and then over the back pockets of his jeans. Her breath quickened as she felt his lips slide down her neck, and his hands grip her hips.

Adam backed Beth up so she was leaning against the nearest tree and moved his hands slowly down her side until he got to the hem of her shirt. He pulled it up, inch by inch. She felt exposed, but her skin was flushed with heat. Adam gently cupped her breasts with his hands, still kissing her neck. Beth was so overwhelmed by desire, she was surprised she had the sense to stop him by grabbing his wrists.

"I'm sorry," he whispered.

"Not here," Beth whispered back, looking toward the cottages. "Someone might see."

And then she took his hand and led him deeper into the forest.

21

Jeremy smelled like soap and something just short of spicy. His eyes were dark and mysterious, and his smile was so adorable Ella could hardly sit still when he turned it on her.

"You look nice," he said, gazing across the table at her. It was Wednesday night, and she and Jeremy were out at a pizza place, on what she was thinking of as a halfway date.

"So do you," Ella replied. The more she looked at him, the more the hidden hotness took over. And she knew she was looking pretty hot, too, in a tight pink slip dress, her blonde hair styled in a sexy mass of curls.

"I'd like to get to know you better," Jeremy said, leaning on the table with sincere interest. It wasn't just a pickup line; he meant it.

"Not much to know," Ella said slyly. "I'm the usual Catholic schoolgirl." She knew that when she said it so sexily, boys tended to go glassy-eyed.

But Jeremy just smiled, and traced a pattern on the red-and-white-checked tablecloth with his index finger. "What's Catholic school like?" he asked.

"You mean when we're not tying up our shirts and dirty-dancing in the hallways?"

"Uh, I guess." Jeremy shrugged.

Apparently he wasn't a big Britney fan.

"What's it like to have nuns around, and stuff? Are they really strict?" he asked.

Ella was thrown. It seemed like Jeremy might actually *care* about the details of her life. He really wanted to learn about what made her tick. This was new.

"Well, Sister Margaret Alice is a sadist," she groaned before taking a sip of her Diet Coke. "But you know, the more rules and regulations there are, the more fun it is to break them."

"Like in *Heaven Help Us*," Jeremy said eagerly, his eyes lighting up again. He looked down at his plate when Ella shrugged. "It's this really cool movie from, like, the eighties. It's about a bunch of kids in Catholic school."

"You really like eighties movies, don't you?"

Ella always wanted to see the latest blockbuster, not stuff from before she was born. But this quirk was cute.

"What's not to like?" He sat back in his chair. "Come on, you're not allowed to be a teenager unless you've seen *The Breakfast Club*. It's, like, *required.*"

"I've seen *that*," Ella said. She was enthralled by this side of him.

"I don't know why John Hughes stopped making movies,"

Jeremy said, tearing off a piece of bread. "The man was a genius."

The pizza came then, and Ella soon found herself giggling over their shared inability to eat without dribbling cheese and sauce.

"Not the best food to eat in front of a girl," Jeremy said, wiping at a stain he'd gotten on his long-sleeved T-shirt.

Ella laughed, and counted herself lucky that she had managed to avoid dripping tomato sauce all over herself. Given the extreme klutziness she seemed to suffer around this guy, she couldn't believe she hadn't upended the entire pizza into her lap.

After dinner, they walked a little way down the street and stopped at one of the scenic spots that overlooked the beach, with a bench to enjoy the view. Ella mindlessly took Jeremy's hand as they leaned against the railing. Things felt so natural between them.

"What do you want to do now?" he asked, smiling at her as his fingers tightened around hers. "I think some people are having a bonfire down on the beach tonight. There's a Jet Li marathon at the Royale, if you feel like some kung fu. Or we could go somewhere else."

Ella was just enjoying the sound of his voice and how comfortable he seemed to be with her now, so she barely heard the options. "Um," she said. "What was that?"

"I know I'm going to sound so stupid when I say this," Jeremy whispered. "But you really are the prettiest girl I've ever seen."

Then he inhaled very deeply, pulled her closer, and kissed her. Just a light touch of his lips. It was so delicate and sweet that Ella's heart swelled with sheer joy.

About time!

She stroked the side of Jeremy's face as she kissed him back. She parted his lips with her tongue, and he didn't resist. Ella was delighted when one of his arms snaked around her waist. He turned them both around, still kissing her, and Ella walked backward until she felt the bench behind her. Then Jeremy pulled away briefly to smile at her, before leading her down to cradle her in his lap.

Ella didn't know how long they sat like that, kissing as if they were all alone in the world. She loved how his lips had the slight hint of Coke to them, and the feel of his arms around her. She felt a jolt of excitement race along her skin when he smoothed his hands down her arms. This was perfect. But Ella still decided to take it up a notch. While her tongue tangled with his, she let her hand trail down his fantastic abdomen, marveling at its flatness. Then, feeling invincible, she reached down just a little bit farther south, and gave him a quick and naughty squeeze.

She expected Jeremy to react. All the boys she'd ever been with had gone nuts after she'd touched them like that. It was a surefire boy-pleaser.

But she didn't expect the reaction she got: Jeremy yanked her hand away, looking nervous and weird instead of turned on and excited.

"What?" she whispered seductively.

"Uh, I should probably head back," he said.

"Why?"

This wasn't supposed to happen.

He gently shifted her off his lap, then stood, putting his hands in his pockets.

"I'll walk you home," Jeremy said, then turned and trudged ahead.

It took about thirty seconds for Ella to realize that he was serious. And then another thirty seconds to feel her face heat up. All her other humiliations with him were *nothing* compared to this moment.

"Are you coming?" Jeremy asked, from a safe distance.

Ella glared at him, and got to her feet.

"No, I'm going out to meet some people," she said dismissively. So what if she was lying? There was no way she was going to let this guy mess with her dignity, which was already on its last legs.

Jeremy sighed. "Ella, wait."

But she swept by him without another word. She didn't know where she was going, but Ella just knew she had to get far away from him.

A few minutes later, Ella arrived on Main Street and was surprised to discover that, for once, she didn't feel like joining in the noise and hubbub. She saw a line forming outside Ahoy, and for the first time in, like, forever, she didn't feel like dancing. She strolled farther down the street and smiled at the bouncers outside the Lighthouse, but she felt far too demoralized to even try talking her way in.

She had just passed the entrance to the bar when she saw him. He was walking down the street, his head tilted down toward a petite brunette. It was the way he walked that first caught Ella's attention. She remembered it so well: slow and deliberate and confident.

Peter.

He was still tall and slender, and astoundingly hot. The stray fantasies she'd had about him getting fat or ugly hadn't come true at all. He still had that vibe about him — the one that screamed, "I'm irresistible!" When he laughed, his black eyes seemed to glow.

Ella wondered if she'd lost her poise with this guy somehow. She'd wasted it on him, and now she was getting rejected — something that had never happened to her before. It was like Peter had cursed her.

Without really thinking, Ella stepped behind a group of tourists outside the restaurant next door. Peter seemed enthralled by the girl next to him, and she was as overwhelmed and gushy as Ella imagined any girl would be at his side. Ella felt a low throb in her abdomen.

Something reckless inside her bloomed then. She should just walk over there and interrupt him with his latest conquest. Make a move on him and see what happened. *Why not?* He was still texting her all the time. She knew that he, at least, wanted *her.* So why shouldn't she have him?

But she'd taken no more than a step or two, her eyes still on him, when Ella paused. Peter ushered the brunette ahead of him into the Lighthouse. And the minute the girl couldn't see him, he locked eyes with the redhead standing by the door. Ella watched him lean in close and whisper something, and she didn't have to hear what he said to guess it was the reason the redhead started smiling. That or his hand, which squeezed the redhead's butt as he angled his way past her.

Peter's sexy grin spread across his face.

None the wiser, the brunette kept on walking.

And that, Ella realized, *is the guy you betrayed your sister for.*

She turned away from the lights and the music, and kept on walking.

"There you are."

Beth's voice came out of the darkness, scaring Ella as she was creeping into her house. She jumped, her hand dropping from the door of the cottage, and turned to blink at her cousin.

"What are you doing out here in the dark?" she demanded. "You scared the —"

"I have to talk to you," Beth said nervously.

Something was definitely up.

"Okay," Ella said suspiciously, and followed Beth out into the yard.

"I don't know where to start," Beth said. Ella saw that her face was flushed and her eyes were swimming with tears. "I don't understand how this happened." She looked at Ella, then hugged herself tightly. "I just . . . cheated on George. With Adam." Her voice was squeaky.

"Um, okay," Ella said. Her own surreal night paled in

comparison to *that* bombshell. She steered Beth over to the picnic tables and sat her down with a gentle push. "Wait right here."

"Where are you going?" Beth asked.

"To get reinforcements," Ella replied calmly.

When she returned, Beth hadn't moved a muscle, and Ella had two huge mugs of hot chocolate topped with whipped cream.

Beth took the mug Ella offered her, and sighed.

"Drink up," Ella said. "But I should warn you, I added some special ingredients." Beth's eyes widened. "Relax, just extra marshmallows," Ella said with a giggle. *And some whiskey from Dad's liquor cabinet,* she thought.

"You know," Beth said in a rush, "you don't have to listen to this. I mean, I know I've been kind of cold to you lately. El, I totally judged you for the Peter thing and there's no reason you should even pay attention to *my* problems. . . ."

"Drink your hot chocolate," Ella ordered, rolling her eyes.

Beth's lips trembled. She was trying not to cry. But she took Ella's advice and drank from her mug. Ella did the same.

"This is actually pretty good," Beth murmured. "But there's something else in here besides marshmallows," she accused.

Ella just shrugged. "Listen to Dr. Ella, okay? Drink up."

Beth's eyes filled with tears again. "I'm so glad you're here, El."

"I won't judge you," Ella said simply. "Now, start at the beginning."

*   *   *

At exactly nine thirty-two, Ella stumbled out into the gray morning and flung her duffel bag down next to the car. She felt like flinging herself to the ground along with it, but the grass was wet with dew. Up above, the sun was just starting to burn off the clouds, which meant that it was still cold. Ella wrapped her hooded waffle-knit sweatshirt around herself and zipped it up to the chin.

"What?" Ella asked hoarsely when Kelsi glared at her. She wondered if she shouldn't be wearing her sunglasses when there was no sunlight. But it was too late to take them off — Kelsi had already noticed. Whatever. Sunlight or no sunlight, it was way too bright after a night full of tears, talk, and seriously spiked cocoa.

"You're totally hung over, aren't you?" Kelsi hissed. "Typical."

Ella shrugged. She was far too exhausted to defend herself to her sister. She stuck a piece of gum in her mouth and wondered when the handful of Advil she'd just downed was likely to start contending with her headache. This was what happened when you tried to be sympathetic. Next time she had to be up at dawn, she should not stay awake until almost six in the morning. But how could she turn away a cousin in need?

"I thought we called a truce," Ella said then.

"Whatever," Kelsi snapped. She pointed a finger at a square-shouldered figure walking up the road. "My friend Tim is here. Behave yourself."

As Tim drew closer, Ella was pleased to see that this "friend" of Kelsi's wasn't one of those hippie types she usually befriended, dressed in hemp and sporting knotted dreads. No, this guy was downright . . . sexy.

"Check out your boyfriend," Ella said, impressed. "He's gorgeous, Kelsi."

"Don't even think about it," Kelsi said in a tight, low voice. "Anyway, he's not my boyfriend so you wouldn't get any satisfaction out of doing him, would you?" She walked away to meet Tim in the driveway.

Kelsi's response hurt Ella so much that she actually gasped for breath. She wrestled her bag from the ground into the trunk, and then crawled into the backseat of the car. She was dying for a smoke, but she knew Kelsi would kill her if she tried.

Her head hurt, she felt like throwing up, and she wanted to cry. Okay, Ella *was* crying. But she managed to wipe the tears away and curl into a ball in the backseat so no one could see her face.

22

For the first part of the trip, everyone was quiet, and Kelsi concentrated on the winding roads that led inland from the coast to I-95. Once on the interstate, the drive would be pretty easy, but first there were the slow and curving country routes to navigate. The morning was cool and fog pooled in the hollows and the woods, but the sky seemed to be clearing far in the distance.

Tim lounged in the passenger seat and seemed to be involved with the scenery, and Kelsi could hear blessed silence coming from the backseat, where Ella had sprawled across the entire width of the car and buried her head in her sweatshirt. She'd been fast asleep before Kelsi had even pulled out of the driveway.

Kelsi privately hoped that she'd stay like that the entire way down to Amherst and — hey — maybe the whole time they were there, too. She knew she'd been the one to suggest a truce, but she was already rethinking the whole idea. Ella's instant appreciation of Tim totally rubbed Kelsi the wrong way. Not to mention her obvious hangover. For all Kelsi knew, it was because she'd been out all night reacquainting herself with Peter the Jerk.

She realized she was clenching her jaw and forced herself to stop.

An hour or so later, the sun was out and streaming into the car, but Kelsi was still simmering with anger.

No longer slumped in his seat, Tim was swiveled half around so he could look at Ella in the backseat. Because, Kelsi fumed silently, that was what all guys did when they were anywhere near Ella. Her sister had woken up and seemed — as far as Kelsi could tell — all too eager to chatter away with Tim. Kelsi had watched Ella covertly in the rearview mirror as soon as Tim turned to her.

First, she'd taken out her sloppy ponytail, and smoothed her lush golden hair. Then she'd unzipped her hoodie, revealing a clingy blue tank top. Soon, she'd magically managed to gloss her lips so they shone, and she was laughing at everything Tim said. Then she was leaning forward between the two front seats, like Tim was some irresistible lure. The two of them seemed to be getting along so well that Kelsi was tempted to pull the car over to the side of the road and let herself out. She could walk the rest of the way to Amherst and the two of them could have more privacy to continue their annoying argument about who was more cheesy: Britney or Christina.

"Christina may have started off trashy, but you have to

admit, Britney's decline has been truly spectacular," Tim argued with a big smirk. In any other situation, Kelsi might have smiled along or even laughed. Right now, she just felt pissed, a feeling that intensified when Ella shrieked loudly from the backseat.

"Whatever," Ella retorted. "Britney is still my girl. I don't care how many freaky pimp boyfriends she marries."

"That's your argument?" Tim shook his head. "Pathetic. Next thing, you're going to trot out the absurd 'Justin broke her heart' defense."

Ella practically screamed at that. "Oh my God, you can't even go there, he *totally* broke her heart and then *sold her out* —"

"And I thought *she* cheated on the poor guy," Tim interrupted.

"But it's all teenage drama," Ella said. "Everyone knows they're meant for each other. It doesn't matter how many times she gets married, or how long he dates movie stars. It's *destiny.*"

The star-crossed love between Justin Timberlake and Britney Spears was a topic that had never interested Kelsi. Ella, meanwhile, talked like she was personally invested in the stars' reunion. Kelsi had heard this rant from Ella so many times that she could probably recite it. She barely even heard the words anymore. But Tim, she noticed, seemed to be hanging on to every one.

Gritting her teeth — again — Kelsi tried to focus on the road.

After all, why should she care if Tim found Ella as delightful as every other guy in the entire world seemed to find her?

He wasn't her boyfriend. He was barely her friend. Why should she care what he did?

She was still pondering that question a while later when they pulled into a rest stop in Massachusetts for food, gas, and a restroom break.

"Want me to drive?" Ella asked. She was holding the big bottle of Classic Coke and family pack of Dentyne Ice she'd just purchased.

"I'm fine," Kelsi said crisply. She returned the nozzle to its place on the pump. Definitely with more aggression than the action warranted.

"You've been driving all morning," Ella said, slightly hesitant. "I can take over."

If Kelsi didn't know better, she might have thought that Ella was actually trying to be helpful, even sensitive to someone else's needs.

Obviously, this was some sort of elaborate trick.

"I said I was fine," Kelsi snapped.

She watched Ella blink, and then rock back on her heels a bit. Kelsi noticed that, under her tiny blue spaghetti-strap tank top, Ella wasn't wearing a bra. *Typical,* Kelsi thought angrily. And all for Tim's benefit, naturally.

"Your friend is really cool," Ella said in a voice Kelsi recognized as cautious.

Good, she thought. *You* should *be more careful.*

"He's all right," Kelsi told her. "For a frat boy moron."

And because her life was just that ridiculous, Tim was standing right behind her when she said that. Kelsi saw Ella's mouth sort of drop open, but before she could react, she heard Tim's amused chuckle.

"Sad but true," he told Ella, shaking his head. "It's all keggers and football for me — I'm so ashamed."

Kelsi felt her face go red, but when she turned to look, *Tim* didn't look ashamed at all. He looked smirky and entertained, the way he always did. Kelsi was the one who felt ashamed, but she told herself it was just anger, and crawled back behind the wheel.

"Are you sure —" Ella began.

"Ella, get in the car!" Kelsi barked at her, turning the key in the ignition. "The last time I let you drive me somewhere, you almost got arrested."

"It was a speeding ticket!" Ella protested, but she climbed into the backseat and slammed the door shut. "And that cop just had it in for me because, hello, we were so much cuter than she was."

"Yeah, and I'm sure she really enjoyed it when you pointed that out to her," Kelsi said. "I promised Dad there would be no moving violations on this road trip, okay?"

"I can't believe she blames me for that," Ella said, turning her attention back to Tim. She hardly looked hung over anymore, Kelsi noticed. The mere presence of a boy instantly reenergized her. It was infuriating.

"*She* nearly had to spend the night in jail," Kelsi chimed in bitterly. "Funny how that made it all just slightly less entertaining."

"She is such a freaking killjoy," Ella told Tim in a slightly lowered voice, leaning over the seat a bit more. "Let me tell you what happened and you can decide. It'll be like on *American Idol*."

"Excellent," Tim said. "I've always wanted to be Simon Cowell. Can I tell you exactly what I think, no-holds-barred?"

"Of course!" Ella said, with a giggle. "I'm not afraid of the truth."

Why can't they just do each other and get it over with? Kelsi wondered furiously. Anyone watching this scene would have thought that Kelsi and Tim hardly knew each other, and *Ella* and Tim were the couple. Not that Kelsi cared about Tim. Or did she? It was her own fault for letting down her guard with him — which she would never have done if she hadn't found out about Ella and Peter. It seemed all roads led back to how evil Ella was.

But did Tim really have to be *that* into her?

Kelsi just kept her eyes on the road and somehow restrained herself from murdering her sister and the irritating boy next to her.

She couldn't get to Amherst fast enough.

When Beth finally woke up, she thought she might have died.

Then she remembered what had happened last night and she sort of wished she *had* died.

She managed to disentangle herself from the stranglehold of her floral bedsheets, and looked around her bedroom in sleepy confusion. The room was hot, and light streamed in through the windows. The clock announced that it was already afternoon. And her cell phone showed that there were no missed calls.

Somehow, that last part was the most ominous.

It was as if George somehow knew. As if he had *just known* last evening, the way people in movies always seemed to bolt awake in the middle of the night with premonitions of plane crashes or assassinations.

Beth stood in the shower for a long time, tilting her face directly into the water and hoping it might wash away all the things she felt. Not that her hangover was too terrible. That, at least, numbed some of the memory. But not all of it.

She'd kissed Adam. So many times. And then she'd done more than that. In a small, dark clearing in the woods, they'd been all over each other. Adam had removed her shirt and bra, and Beth shivered in the shower, remembering how he'd stripped them from her in nearly one hasty, rough motion. They'd sunk to the ground together, kissing nonstop. His hands had been everywhere, stroking and caressing every inch of bare skin. It had felt so amazing. So exciting. Within minutes, he'd taken off his jeans. But when Beth slipped her hand under the waistband of his boxers, she realized the seriousness of what was happening. Kissing was one thing, but if she let this boil over, it would turn into something much more intense. And she couldn't let that happen.

I didn't have sex with him, Beth reminded herself. *I didn't let it go too far.*

But they'd gone far enough.

She closed her eyes.

George.

How could she have allowed this? What did this say about her relationship with George? How could she be so in love with George — and she did think she still loved him, even now — yet have kissed Adam the way she'd kissed him last night?

Beth turned off the faucets and climbed out of the shower. Sooner or later, she had to face the day.

After a defiantly big breakfast of bacon and eggs, she took

a long run. When she got back, winded and sweaty, she wandered around the cottage and wondered what in the world to do with herself. Ella and Kelsi were probably already in Amherst, having fun with Jamie. George still hadn't called, thankfully. Since he hadn't gotten in touch with her, it probably meant he wasn't coming up this weekend after all and wanted to avoid another fight over the phone. Which meant that *she* could have gone to Amherst. And if she'd known that in advance, there was a really big chance that instead of hanging around with Adam, she would have been too busy packing for the trip. Which meant she would never have fooled around with him. So really, it was George's fault. If he wasn't so flaky, none of this would have happened.

She tried really hard to believe that one, concentrating on it fiercely for a few minutes, but it wouldn't take.

Beth knew exactly whose fault it was.

Me, myself, and I.

A few minutes later, her phone rang.

Adam.

Beth looked at his name on her phone's little screen and sighed, putting it aside without answering.

It hadn't really sunk in yet, she realized then. That *of course* he would call the next day. He thought things had changed between them now. Maybe he thought they were dating or something. Beth panicked a little bit.

Who cares what Adam thinks, or what George thinks? Ella had counseled the night before, surprisingly wise. *What do you* think?

In fact, Ella had been surprising all the way through. She'd really seemed to get Beth's confusion and the depth of her anguish. Beth hadn't expected that. She'd thought Ella would only care about whether or not Adam was a good hook up (which, *oh God,* he was). But instead, her cousin had seemed to absolutely understand why things had gotten so difficult and crazy for Beth. How Beth had felt like she couldn't really help herself. And, true to her word, Ella hadn't judged.

Bethy, she'd said at one point, when Beth couldn't speak through the sobs. *The fact is, feelings are gonna be hurt here. You just have to figure out how you can make yourself happy, and you should be honest about it. That's really what matters.*

Oddly, that was the most comforting thing she'd said. *Be honest,* Beth told herself now, when the phone rang yet again, and Adam's number flashed across the screen.

But, regardless, she couldn't quite bring herself to answer the call.

By the time they reached Amherst, Kelsi wanted to kick Tim
out of the car. While it was still moving, if possible.

The asshole.

It wasn't just that he continued to engage Ella in conversation, so that Kelsi had to hear her treacherous little sister giggle
and flirt and almost audibly bat her eyelashes. It was the *way*
he did it. He seemed as if he was just as enchanted by every
single inane thing that fell from Ella's mouth as all the rest of
the stupid boys out there.

When she finally pulled onto the U Mass campus, Kelsi
decided that she was thrilled that Tim was finally getting out of
the car and — she could only hope — her life. He'd told her to
trust him, and she'd known better, hadn't she? Next time she
planned to heed her gut instinct.

Tim climbed out of the car and stretched, a move which
showed off the swath of tan skin between the top of his jeans

and the bottom his T-shirt. Kelsi tossed her door open and then stormed around to the trunk of the car. As she flung it open, she was glad that, for once, Ella seemed to be more interested in the state of her nails than in the nearest cute boy. The windows of the car were rolled down, but Ella didn't seem to be paying attention to Kelsi or Tim.

"Okay," Tim said, coming around to haul his duffel bag from the trunk. He smiled at Kelsi like everything was great and he didn't deserve to be drop-kicked with full *Kill Bill* force. "I guess I'll —"

"Go to hell?" Kelsi suggested nastily, cutting him off.

He paused. "What?" he asked, obviously hoping he'd just misheard her.

"Have a nice weekend," Kelsi snapped. "And you can find yourself a new ride back up to Pebble Beach. I don't think I could stomach five more minutes of you, much less five more hours."

"Wow." Tim settled his bag over one shoulder. There was no sign of his smirk or his usual amusement. Instead, his eyes looked dim. "That's pretty cold, Kelsi, even for you."

"What's that supposed to mean?" she demanded.

"It means that you think you're entitled to say any rude thing that crosses your mind, and you expect me to keep laughing it off!" For the first time since she'd known him, Tim seemed dead serious. It sounded like that thought had been building up inside him, because his voice rose a little — but Kelsi was too mad to care.

"Let me assure you, I don't have any expectations as far as

you're concerned," she shot back. Like *she* was the rude one! He was so clueless!

"Yeah, you've made that pretty clear," he said coolly. "I don't know why I wasted my time."

His voice sounded weirdly bitter, which made Kelsi wish she hadn't yelled at him — but only for a brief second. He'd been flirting with Ella right under her nose, she reminded herself, when he of all people *knew* how that would make her feel.

"Whatever." She glared at him, willing him to apologize. But he just looked back at her and said nothing. "I guess I'll see you around."

"I wouldn't count on it," Tim replied. And then, just like that, he turned and walked away.

Kelsi watched him go for a moment, then slammed the trunk closed with all her might — so hard she actually made her hand throb. When she climbed back into the car, Ella had crawled over into the front seat, and was sneaking looks Kelsi's way while she finished filing her nails.

"What?" Kelsi said aggressively.

"What was that all about?" Ella asked, sounding amazed and confused at the same time. "Why were you so mad at him?"

"Just shut up," Kelsi spoke through her teeth. "Call Jamie and tell her we're almost there."

"But —"

"I'm serious!" Kelsi said. "I don't want to hear another word about Tim from you, of all people!"

Ella made a face, but she didn't argue any further. She

fished out her phone, and Kelsi had to restrain herself from snatching the thing out of her sister's hand and seeing for herself if her ex was still busy texting sweet nothings Ella's way.

But she did nothing of the kind. She just gritted her teeth as her sister chattered away with Jamie, as if Ella hadn't just spent the entire morning sucking up to yet another guy in Kelsi's life. As if Tim wasn't just one more heartless jock jerk.

As if everything was just fine and dandy.

Ella had never been so excited to see her cousin Jamie in her life.

Jamie was waiting for them on the steps in front of her dorm, her black hair piled high on her head in her trademark messy bun, her green eyes dancing when she spotted the car.

"Finally!" she cried. "I can't believe how much I missed you guys!"

"We missed you, too!" Kelsi called, with a big smile and without the slightest indication that she'd completely lost her mind a short while before.

Ella was confused by her sister. The fight with Tim had come out of nowhere. He was adorable, sweet, and, if Ella was still able to read guys right (despite the Jeremy debacle), he was totally into Kelsi. Shows what Kelsi knew. Now Ella was so relieved that Jamie was around. Ella knew that Kelsi was unlikely to get all psycho in front of sweet, soothing Jamie.

Ella gave her cousin a huge hug and grinned at her. Everything about Jamie was just so . . . *Jamie*. The mess of freckles. The sloppy hair. The bohemian-chic look she was sporting. Ella felt a rush of love and kissed her cousin on the cheek.

"We've been driving forever," she cried. "Let's start the party!"

Can't I just take a nap? Ella wondered several hours later, trudging up a hill with Jamie and Kelsi.

Jamie was so excited about spending her summer in Amherst that she'd taken her cousins on a walking tour of the *whole freaking town.* Sure, Amherst was pretty. There was a big green square in the center, and the college sat up on top of a hill looking down on it all. It would make a lovely postcard, and Ella wished Jamie had just sent them one instead of making them *ooh* and *aah* over every square inch.

Jamie checked her watch and gasped. "It's late!" she said. "We're supposed to meet some friends of mine back at the dorm."

"Sounds great," Ella said excitedly. That sounded a whole lot more fun than anything else they'd done all day. Not that Ella didn't enjoy hanging out with Jamie, of course. She just wasn't one for extended walking tours. For one thing, she was wearing the wrong shoes. But what else was new?

Ella just smiled serenely when Kelsi sent a suspicious look her way, like she knew exactly what Ella was thinking.

Jamie led them back toward her dorm, pointing out various sights along the way. Ella tuned out and wondered what

Jamie's writer friends would be like. She had a pretty good idea that the level of hotness would be fairly low. After all, these people were, by choice, spending their summer trapped indoors, doing what Ella thought of as schoolwork. Who *chose* to go to summer school?

They had to climb up five flights of stairs to get to Jamie's tiny little room with its slanted ceiling and single window. Ella thought the place looked like a jail cell and, if this was what college was going to be like, she had some serious doubts. Maybe she'd just learn cosmetology. She definitely had enough self-taught beauty skills.

"It's my own little garret," Jamie said, grinning as if she'd actually picked this room out of all the others.

"I definitely need to shower if we're going out," Ella announced, gesturing to her rumpled clothes and hair. "I can't meet new people looking like this."

"Yeah, because that would really hold you back," Kelsi said with a snort. There was a small silence, while Jamie looked from one sister to the other.

"Um," Jamie said carefully. "We should all shower, then. I feel kind of grimy, too."

The three of them gathered towels, soap, and shampoo, and trotted down the long corridor toward the hall bathroom.

"I can't believe you have to share a bathroom with so many people," Ella said with a shudder. "Doesn't it get gross?"

"That's why you wear flip-flops in the shower," Kelsi said mockingly. She swept back the curtain of the nearest shower and turned the water on.

"The *boys'* dorms are disgusting," Jamie said, shifting another curious glance from Kelsi to Ella. "But this is a girls' dorm. Much cleaner."

The girls all stepped into the three curtained stalls. Ella sighed with pleasure as the steam and hot water poured over her.

"So," Jamie called out over the roar of the water. "Tell me *everything* that's going on in Maine. When Beth e-mails me, she leaves all the good parts out, but I know you guys would never do something like that."

"Ask Ella about *everything*," Kelsi shouted snidely.

In the privacy of her stall, Ella repeatedly gave her sister the finger.

"It's true, I believe in spreading gossip to those less fortunate," Ella agreed theatrically. "Where should I start?"

"Beth," Jamie said immediately. "Definitely. What's the deal with that lifeguard guy? What about George? It's all scandalous, and she hasn't answered my last *three* e-mails!"

Ella was only too happy to spill the details of someone else's bad decisions, of course. Particularly if it helped avoid a discussion of her own — which she worried Kelsi was about one more obnoxious comment away from beginning.

"Well," Ella began, running the vanilla shower gel along her arms and enjoying the way her voice echoed in the tiled room. The longer she kept talking, the more likely it was she could keep Kelsi from erupting like Mount Saint Helens. "Our cousin Beth has been a little too busy to answer any e-mails. . . ."

26

Adam had stopped calling, and turned up at the cottage early on Saturday morning instead. For once, Beth was grateful for her parents' interference. Her mother had told him she was still in bed — factually correct, although she hadn't been asleep — and even someone as determined as Adam didn't try to argue his way past her mom.

Beth knew he had to work all day, so she figured he'd be easy enough to keep avoiding. She spent the afternoon wallowing at home, which was so far removed from her usual way of dealing with things that Beth knew she was in serious trouble. She picked up the phone at least a hundred times to call George, but couldn't make herself hit the SEND button. If she got ahold of George, and didn't tell him about Adam, she would officially become the Worst Person Ever.

Looking back over the summer, Beth could see that she

should have paid more attention to Ella's teasing — all the G-2 comments — but she'd been in serious denial about her feelings for Adam all along. It seemed to her now that she'd started to fall for him the moment she'd looked up from the ocean current to see him pull his Jet Ski up next to her.

As evening crept in, Beth roused herself and set out for a walk. She thought she might hang out on the beach down by the pier, where it would be dark and anonymous and she could keep on brooding. Also, she was pretty sure that Adam might try to drop in on her again, and she didn't think she could face him just yet. Or maybe not ever. She supposed that made her a total coward. But part of her was hoping that if she never saw Adam again, that would somehow erase what had happened between them. If they didn't have the inevitable big discussion about it, then *it* wouldn't be real.

Beth was clinging to that.

She pulled on a baseball cap and a fleece against the cool evening air, and snuck away from the cottages without calling attention to herself. She could hear her family gathering around the barbecue, the way they always did, and she felt the sudden, lonely sting of self-pity. She didn't feel like she belonged there anymore. Beth had this not-so-irrational fear that they'd all be able to see that she was someone else, all of a sudden. Someone who would do what she'd done to George.

Swallowing the lump in her throat, Beth turned and headed down the dirt road. Once she was out of sight of the cottages, she suddenly found herself face-to-face with Adam.

Her heart jumped. Beth hugged herself around the middle, as if that might give her some relief. She just didn't know what to say to this boy she'd spent the entire summer with, and whose body she'd just explored with so much enthusiasm. He seemed like a stranger to her now.

"You're avoiding me," he said, his blue eyes dark with emotion.

Beth couldn't deny that, so she just shrugged and rocked back on her heels. She felt like sprinting down the road and off into the night until she reached the coastline, yet at the same time she felt paralyzed.

"Look," Adam said, stepping closer. "I know that maybe things went kind of far last night. . . ."

Beth cleared her throat and fought down the sudden searing heat of tears. "Adam, I have a boyfriend," she whispered, unnecessarily. "And I love him. I can't hurt him."

But did she? Did she love George? How could she know anymore?

"I get that," Adam said impatiently. "But I can't pretend I'm not happy about what happened. I wanted it to happen all summer."

"But it was wrong," Beth said then, turning away. "For me." She sighed. "I never should have . . ." She shook her head, as if to clear it. "After we kissed that first time, I should have just stayed away from you."

"But you didn't." Adam followed her, not letting her keep her back to him. "And what happened was amazing, Beth. You know it was."

Beth didn't know how to respond. It was true. But how could she even let herself admit that?

"I know you're confused," Adam said, sounding kind of desperate. "But we really have something special, Beth. I've never been this into a girl. I can't talk to anyone the way I can talk to you. I think I'm in —"

"We shouldn't even be having this conversation!" Beth cut him off and took a step back, terrified by the prospect of what he was starting to say. "As much as I want to, I can't go back and undo everything. But I *can* prevent it from happening again. I can't hang out with you anymore, Adam. We never should have crossed that line, but we did, and now I need you to stay away from me."

"I can't do that!" Adam replied, his voice heavy with emotion. "I don't *want* to do that. And I don't think you do, either. You should give us a chance, Beth. Don't you think we at least deserve that?"

"I . . ." Beth stared up at his mouth, the mouth she had kissed so many times. She wished she could delete the memory of their hook up from her brain, so when she looked at him, she would feel none of this temptation or wistfulness.

"I know you feel the way I do," Adam said softly, studying her face. "I can feel it."

Beth reached up, and then dropped her hand to her side. It would be foolish to touch him. She knew that.

As if he read her mind, he reached over and held her shoulders, massaging them a little bit.

"Don't throw this away," he urged again, with a glimmer of

his smile. "We're friends, we have fun together, and Beth, you're . . . incredible. In every way."

The night was drawing in close and Beth felt that same weakness flood her. Why was he so captivating? The urge to touch him tingled through her fingertips. She took a step closer to Adam, and he lowered his head toward her . . .

Suddenly, she saw a figure waver in the shadows behind Adam. She blinked and looked closer, and for a long moment couldn't make sense of what she saw.

George stood there in the middle of the dirt road. He'd obviously just walked up, on his way to the cottages.

Beth had never seen that particular look on his face before, like all the humor and spirit that made George who he was had completely drained out of him. Some stranger, some other George, stood there, with dead eyes. She wasn't sure she could bear to look at him, but she couldn't seem to turn away. She was aware of too many things at once — Adam's hands on her shoulders, how close they were standing, how George must have understood everything in one heartbeat.

"George . . ." Beth whispered, not even sure she was speaking out loud.

Adam turned, too, and then all three of them were standing there, staring at one another. Beth thought she could hear the tide pounding against the beach, but then realized that was just the blood roaring in her ears.

George was holding a huge bouquet of flowers. Yellow tulips, her favorite.

"Surprise," George said flatly.

Still holding Beth's gaze, he dropped the flowers in the dirt at his feet, then turned and walked away. When he was gone and out of view, all she could think was:

What have I done?

27

Ella and Kelsi were halfway back to Pebble Beach when the tire blew out. First there was a loud banging noise, then the car started wobbling ferociously.

This is just terrific! Kelsi thought furiously.

It had been a long, strange weekend. It had been wonderful to see Jamie, as always. She was obviously in her element with all her new writer friends. It was nice to see someone so happy, but it had the unfortunate side effect of making Kelsi think about why she herself felt so unhappy. There was the Ella–Peter thing, of course, which shrouded everything in a foul smog, but Kelsi found that she spent most of the weekend thinking about the look on Tim's face when she'd left him at U Mass.

It hadn't helped that Ella had, predictably, overslept on Sunday morning and they'd gotten a much later start than

Kelsi had wanted. She'd been silently seething about that for hours. And there was no reason for the truce any longer, now that the weekend was over. The more miles Kelsi put between them and Amherst, the more she fumed about everything.

When the tire blew, she drove the car over to the side of the road. Luckily, traffic was light and their ordeal felt less hair-raising than it might have if they had been stuck in the usual weekend commute rush hour. This didn't prevent Ella, who had either been passed out or faking it really well, from jolting upright and screaming like the drama queen she was.

"That's not really helpful," Kelsi told her. The car rolled to a stop, and Ella held a hand over her heart in what Kelsi thought was a needless gesture. Like she was some affronted Southern belle or something.

"Well, excuse me," Ella snapped. "The next time we almost die in the middle of a highway, I'll try to behave more appropriately!"

Those words were the final straw for Kelsi.

It all happened in slow motion: Everything sort of swirled around and then crashed down on her. All the pain she'd been carrying around over Peter, which hurt so much worse now that she knew Ella's part in it. Ella's sudden friendship over the past year, which seemed almost more upsetting than the initial betrayal last summer, because it was all so *planned* and *coldblooded.* The fight with Tim. Even this past weekend with Jamie — Kelsi had felt so isolated and left out. She was losing her mind, and it was Ella's fault.

"Like you'd know something about behaving appropriately?" Kelsi yelled at her little sister. "You *fucked* my *boyfriend!*"

That hung there for a moment, true and ugly, between them. Ella stared back at her, her brown eyes wide and stricken.

Suddenly, Kelsi felt guilty, which made her even angrier.

"No response?" she asked. "Why am I not surprised?"

Ella shut her eyes for a moment, then opened them again. "Um, do we have a plan for the tire?" she asked in a neutral tone.

"Are you *ignoring* me?" Kelsi chided her in disbelief. The very idea of Ella trying to take some kind of high road made Kelsi's blood pressure skyrocket.

"What do you want me to say?" Ella shouted, surprising Kelsi with both the volume and emotion in her voice. "You have no idea how bad I feel, and nothing I could say could ever make up for it."

"How about saying you're sorry?" Kelsi slapped her palms against the steering wheel. "Or is that too much for you?"

"Of course I'm sorry." Ella stared at her. "I've been feeling sorry about this every day for the past year. Does that make you feel any better?"

And, of course, it didn't. Kelsi hated that Ella was right.

"You know what, El?" Kelsi was horrified to hear that her voice was quivering. "I guess I would have thought the fact that I'm *your sister* should be more important to you than getting one more notch on your bedpost. It's not like you don't have enough already."

Ella stiffened and her mouth tightened, but she didn't

respond, not even to that last, cruel part. When she did, it was after she took a long, deep breath.

"It wasn't like that," she said quietly. "You always think the worst of me."

Kelsi let out a short laugh. "Maybe that's because you always do the worst things!" she said. "Maybe it's because you're so incredibly selfish that ever since we were kids, you've gone out of your way to ruin anything that makes me happy."

"That is total bullshit!" Ella retorted. "Peter was a mistake. He was a mistake for you, and a mistake for me. We need to get past that. But if you're not happy about other stuff in your life, that's your own problem!"

"God forbid Ella Tuttle take responsibility for any —"

"Give me a break," Ella groaned. "You don't *want* to be happy, Kelsi. You want to sit around and judge everyone around you and feel superior."

"What are you talking about?" Kelsi growled.

"Take Tim for example," Ella said accusingly. "Why did you go all psycho on him? What was *that* about?"

"You were practically crawling all over him!" Kelsi fired back. "I don't want a guy who wants you, Ella. Period. The thought of you stealing another guy from me makes me *sick*."

"*First* of all," Ella said in a low, angry tone, "you were technically broken up with Peter that night when you saw us together, okay? I'm not saying what I did wasn't wrong, but just for the record — you had *broken up*."

"Do you really expect me to believe that you didn't have something going on with him before that night?" Kelsi asked.

Ella ignored her. "And second of all, I couldn't care less about Tim. He's not my type *at all,* and —"

"Right, because suddenly, a hot guy who's alive and within range isn't your type. Whatever, Ella."

"— *and,*" Ella continued, right over Kelsi, "it's not like you were even participating in the conversation. You were too busy sulking and being the big victim, which — hello — you *always* do!"

"Why am I having this conversation with you?" Kelsi asked, but she wasn't even directing her words toward Ella anymore. Her stomach was clenched into a fist, and she was shaking. She lurched forward, threw the door open, and got out. On the highway, cars hurtled past at what seemed like amazing speeds. They left wakes, almost like boats, in the air behind them. Kelsi walked around to glare at the flat tire, and realized there were tears blocking her gaze. Fiercely, she wiped her hand across her eyes to clear them.

She heard the passenger door open and then slam, but she didn't look up. Eventually, Ella's ridiculously high platform sandals appeared in her peripheral vision.

"Do you know how to change a tire?" Kelsi asked numbly. She squinted at her sister quickly, and noticed that she was deliberately looking anywhere but back at Kelsi.

"No." Ella eyed the flat. "Do we even have a spare tire?"

"Dad makes sure we do. He's, like, obsessed."

"How come he's not obsessed with teaching one of us what to *do* with the spare tire?" Ella asked drily.

Kelsi ordered herself not to laugh.

Sighing, she went around to the trunk and opened it, then started shoving things out of the way to access the tire well and the spare within. When she straightened up, lugging the spare tire with her, she found Ella standing in a dramatic hitchhiker position. She had her legs on display and her chest stuck out, and as far as Kelsi could surmise, Ella looked like she was for sale.

"What are you doing?" Kelsi asked, giving a frustrated sigh.

"What does it look like I'm doing?"

"Sorry, I must have missed that issue of *Sluts Quarterly*," Kelsi said.

"Very funny. I don't see any reason why you and I should sit here and kill ourselves putting that thing on wrong."

"So . . . you think sticking your boobs into the road will make someone else do it?"

Ella rolled her eyes. "Duh. That's what boys are for."

"Wow," Kelsi said. "That's really deep, Ella. I'm impressed."

"Check it out," Ella interrupted, sounding smug. She flashed a cat-ate-the-canary grin at Kelsi. "Can I deliver, or what?" She gave her cleavage a quick pat, which made Kelsi roll her eyes.

Kelsi turned slowly and watched a red pickup truck roll to a stop just a few feet away. Inevitably, the buff young cowboy-type behind the wheel was entirely focused on Ella's chest.

"You ladies look like you could use a hand," he said, which Kelsi found so beyond patronizing she almost keeled over with rage, but Ella shot her a warning glance.

"And you look like you have the kind of hands we need," Ella told the guy. He all but preened.

"I can't believe you," Kelsi muttered.

"Watch and learn," Ella shot back, and sashayed over to the guy.

* * *

About fifteen minutes later, Brian the Helping Hand was back in his pickup truck, and the Tuttle sisters had a freshly changed tire. And a phone number scribbled on the back of an old 7-Eleven receipt, which Ella threw carelessly into the ashtray.

Kelsi started the car and pulled back into traffic.

"You can thank me anytime," Ella murmured, still smug.

"Now I *really* can't believe you," Kelsi retorted.

There was silence. Then, somehow, Kelsi found herself smiling. "'Oh, Brian!'" She mimicked Ella's flirtatious simper. "'You're just so *strong*!'"

Ella let out one of her trademark snorts. "Hey," she said, "whatever works. *I* didn't want to change that tire. Did you? We didn't even know where to start."

"'Oh, Brian, I can't believe how masterfully you work those lug nuts!'"

Ella laughed. "I never said *that* — I'm not a complete ditz!"

"You *define* 'ditz,'" Kelsi corrected her. "You do it on purpose."

There was a quiet moment again while Kelsi switched lanes.

"I really am sorry," Ella said quietly. "About Peter, and . . . everything. I wish I could undo it somehow, seriously. I never wanted to hurt you. I'm not even sure how it all got so out of control."

Kelsi thought about that for a moment. "So it was you he was with all summer," she said. "Not that girl from the restaurant, the one who worked with him."

Ella sighed. "No, I think he was sleeping with her, too. Bastard."

"And what about this summer?" Kelsi couldn't seem to stop asking questions, even though she was terrified that the answer was going to hurt her even more. If Peter and Ella had hooked up again this summer, it would be even worse. Maybe because it was closer. Or because she and Ella were closer. "Why was he texting you?"

"I don't know," Ella said. "It came out of nowhere. I think maybe he saw me around town or something."

Kelsi thought she was going to have to see a dentist if she continued to grind her teeth like she was doing. She forced herself to stop.

"And . . . ?" The words came slowly. "Did you . . . see him again?"

"God, no," Ella said, and let out a bark of laughter. "I mean, I saw him in the sense that I looked down a street and saw him being a disgusting sleaze with some poor unsuspecting girl." She told Kelsi about the redhead and the brunette. "But that was it. There's been no actual contact. I swear."

Kelsi felt herself ease up. So Peter hadn't specifically chosen Ella. He was simply a slimeball, and maybe that shouldn't make her feel any better, but it did.

"Don't sleep with any of my boyfriends again," Kelsi said, deadly serious. "Don't even flirt. Just so you understand, if you ever do, I'll never speak to you again. Okay?"

"Okay," Ella whispered. Kelsi thought she might even be crying a little.

"I'm your sister," Ella said weakly after a moment and snuffled a bit. "You think I don't know what that means, but I do."

"I hope that's true," Kelsi said quietly.

After a few minutes, Ella shifted in her seat and looked at Kelsi directly.

"By the way," she said, "I *wasn't* flirting with Tim."

Kelsi bit her lip. "I don't want to talk about Tim."

"Okay." Ella shrugged. "But he wasn't flirting with me, either."

"Ella, I was sitting *right here*," Kelsi snapped at her. "I saw —"

"Who knows about flirting, you or me?" Ella interrupted. "He was funny and he was talkative, but he was *not* flirting with me. He was being friendly. Believe me, I know the difference."

"I don't . . ." Kelsi broke off.

"He's into *you*," Ella said.

"I said I don't want to talk about it!" Kelsi insisted, because when she thought about Tim, something surged inside, and she had the suspicion that it was fear. Fear that he would never talk to her again, or make her laugh, or smirk in that smart-ass way of his. It suddenly seemed that the loss of those things might actually cripple her. And that feeling wasn't something she could even begin to share with Ella.

Though she did kind of like the fact that Ella thought Tim was into her.

"What about you?" Kelsi asked her sister. "You've been out so late every night. I know it's paranoid, but I really did think you and Peter . . ."

Ella gathered her blonde hair back with both hands and groaned.

"A world of no," she said with a sigh. "It was Jeremy, but that's pretty much a total bust. I don't think he likes me much."

"What do you mean?" Kelsi asked.

Ella gave her the rundown on the Jeremy situation, and soon Kelsi was laughing despite herself.

"So," Ella finished, after lots of hand waving and eye rolling, "he obviously thinks I'm like a sexual predator or whatever. Right?"

A cruelness stirred in Kelsi then. She wanted to shrug, and say *Of course not* in that way that meant *Yeah, he does,* just to wound Ella. But Ella clearly cared about Jeremy. For the first time in her life, Kelsi's little sister was seriously in doubt over whether or not a guy was into her. Kelsi could see the flush high on Ella's cheeks and the confusion in her round brown eyes.

Kelsi realized she couldn't bring herself to deliberately hurt Ella. She was starting to understand that her anger toward Ella had almost nothing to do with Peter. It went deeper than that — back to their childhood, when pretty, confident Ella had been the one who got all the attention.

But Ella was just . . . Ella. She couldn't help drawing all the attention her way, or the fact that boys flocked to her. Being mad at Ella for *being Ella* seemed unfair and pointless, Kelsi thought. That would be like yelling at the ocean for its waves.

There was a part of Kelsi that was still angry, but there was a much bigger part that loved her sister, no matter what. And now, she wanted to help her.

"You idiot," Kelsi said, almost fondly. "Have you even thought about being subtle?"

Beth barely let Kelsi and Ella get out of the car before she was spilling every horrible detail of George's discovery right there outside the cottages.

"And now I don't know what to do," she concluded. Beth knew she sounded hysterical, but she couldn't help it. "No one's even seen George since last night and what if he, like, decided to walk back to Boston or something? Anything could happen to him! He could be picked up by some serial killer and —"

"Okay," Ella said, cutting her off. "You need to breathe and think rationally for maybe one minute here."

"I'm sorry," Beth said. She closed her eyes and breathed, but it didn't make her feel any better. She wasn't sure she'd ever feel better. She'd been up all night, and all day she'd alternated between crying on her bed in the fetal position — the one that George was so familiar with — and wandering around Pebble Beach looking for George, ignoring Adam's calls.

"First, we need a drink," Ella declared. "We had a long drive, and you're having a crisis, and I believe I have the perfect cure."

"I can only imagine what that means," Kelsi said, and Ella snorted with laughter. Beth noticed the look they exchanged — friendly and possibly even affectionate. Apparently, they'd done some bridge-building on their road trip, but she didn't have the emotional energy to ask about it.

Ella hoisted up her bag and headed for the house. "Our room in, like, five minutes," she called over her shoulder. "I'm hitting Dad's liquor cabinet."

"So," Kelsi said, crossing her arms and turning to look at Beth directly once the screen door slammed shut behind Ella. "When you say 'Adam,' do you mean the Adam I'm supposedly dating?"

Beth wanted to burst into tears, until she saw Kelsi's smile and realized her cousin was okay with that part. She probably had never really been that into Adam. Beth sighed with relief. At least that was one less person she had betrayed.

Later, Beth and her cousins lounged across the beds in Ella and Kelsi's room. Ella had scored a bottle of vodka, a carton of orange juice, and three glasses, which she'd set out with elaborate ceremony. She began mixing drinks immediately.

"We're lucky Dad never checks his alcohol," Ella said.

"What makes you think he doesn't?" Kelsi asked, taking

her drink from Ella. "I always figured he knows we help ourselves sometimes, but he wants to be the fun dad who lets us do stuff like that in the summer."

Ella stared at her sister. "That's sick."

"But possibly true," Kelsi said, laughing. Ella looked disturbed by the possibility.

"Suddenly," she said, "this is less fun."

"How was Jamie?" Beth asked, swirling her drink around in the glass, wanting to forget about herself for a while.

"She's great," Kelsi said, turning to look at Beth. "I think academic life really agrees with her."

"She thinks you're crazy to pick some random surfer guy over George," Ella added, sipping daintily from her drink. "She said, and I quote, 'But Beth's been in love with George for years.'"

"You told her what happened?" Beth didn't know whether to be outraged or touched.

"Like that's a surprise!" Kelsi laughed, and settled back against her headboard. "Ella thinks it's her duty to be the Tuttle family version of *The Enquirer*."

"Please!" Ella fluttered her lashes dramatically. "I'm *US Weekly*, thank you very much!"

Beth snuck another look at Kelsi. She really did seem okay about Adam, but Beth couldn't help feeling even worse because she hadn't considered her cousin's feelings for even a second. And there she'd been, so quick to judge Ella for basically doing the same thing. Some loyal family member she was.

"Of course, Jamie wants to know about your drama," Ella

was saying. "What else is she going to do? She's in summer school. She's, like, convent girl. She's *pining* for stories from the beach."

"What am I? A soap opera?"

"You said it, Bethy, not me." Ella giggled.

Beth groaned. "You guys. Help me. I want George back, but I keep thinking about Adam. . . ."

"This is actually simple," Kelsi said, assuming her Big Sister voice. "You need to choose the boy for you. George or Adam."

"Ooh!" Ella chimed in, scooting closer on the bed. "We can make a list!"

"How can I just make a choice like that?" Beth asked. "This is pretty major."

"It's like making a college decision," Kelsi said. "You can agonize about all the pros and cons of all the available choices, but then at the end, it's really about which one you just know in your gut is right."

Beth searched herself for an answer, but nothing came. "I think I just . . . I really ruined everything."

All three of them were quiet then, until Ella started fussing around the room, topping off their drinks. Beth had slept so little in the past few nights that she already felt buzzed. It was definitely an improvement from how she'd been feeling earlier, she thought as she took another gulp.

"George hates me," Beth said mournfully. "And I can't really blame him, you know?"

"He loves you," Ella replied, flopping back down on the

bed without spilling her drink. "Come on, Beth. You know that."

Beth thought about that for a minute. She and George had always had this intense affection for each other. It was uncomplicated. Effortless. They were soul mates.

In that moment, it suddenly seemed very clear. All this time, Adam was merely a George proxy. A stand-in, someone she transferred all her feelings to because she was lonely. *G-2, indeed.* Not to say that she wasn't attracted to Adam in his own right. But Beth realized that the connection she had with George was irreplaceable. *George* was irreplaceable.

But would he ever forgive her?

Beth sighed and stared at the contents of her glass. "He *used* to love me. But I keep remembering the look on his face. What he must have thought in that moment . . ." She broke off, and then downed the rest of her drink so quickly her throat burned.

"We need a plan," Kelsi said firmly. "You should rent one of those planes and write an apology in the sky. It's a grand gesture. It should at least get him to talk to you."

"No, no, no!" Ella shook her head. "Nobody reads those things."

"I do." Kelsi was grinning.

"Beth, listen to me," Ella said. "I may not be a genius, but if there's anything I do know about, it's boys. Take it from a girl with experience. You have to go the romantic route. You know, like dinner at that expensive place in town, or some begging in public."

"How is that better than skywriting?" Kelsi asked.

"Will you stop with that?" Ella retorted.

"Oh, because *your* date plan is actually going to work?" Kelsi rolled her eyes. "Bethy, you'd have better luck throwing George in the back of the car and holding him hostage until he promised to talk things out."

"Now that's more like it!" Ella said. She turned to Beth, her eyes bright. "We could totally work that. One of us can drive, and all the other two have to do is jump him and drag him into the car, which shouldn't be too hard 'cause he *is* pretty skinny."

"Guys!" Beth was laughing, grateful to feel tipsy. "I think you're missing the bigger problem," she said, aware she was slurring slightly.

"Have another drink," Ella urged her, passing over the vodka bottle.

"I don't even know where George is," Beth said. "The first thing I need to do is find him."

"Here's my final piece of advice," Ella said wisely. "Let George have his space for a while, but don't give up on him. Believe me, boys are sensitive, but they can take a surprising amount of abuse. He'll forgive you."

But every time Beth remembered the ravaged look in George's eyes, she wasn't so sure.

Tim wasn't the only one with secret places scattered around Pebble Beach, Kelsi thought later that afternoon as she made her way down the side of the bluff on the other side of the cottages. All you had to do was get about a fifth of the way down the rocky outcropping, and there was a comfortable ledge to sit on. Kelsi liked to perch there and watch the schooners go by on the sea below, their sails proud and full against the wind as they headed up the coast to Camden and Bar Harbor.

She was almost to her secret spot when she heard someone cough from down on the ledge. *Great.* All she wanted was to be alone and think, and maybe see a pretty sailboat. And she felt unreasonably annoyed that someone else apparently knew about the place she considered hers and hers alone.

"Hey," George said when Kelsi took that final jump and landed on the ledge, breathing hard. She did a double take, surprised he'd turned up so suddenly.

"Uh, hi," Kelsi said. She brushed the dirt off of her hands. "I didn't know anyone knew about this hideout."

"Beth and I followed you here once a couple summers ago," George said with a faint smile. "Sorry."

"No problem," Kelsi said. She went and sat next to him, crossing her legs and staring out at the water. There was just the faintest breeze, bringing the smell of pine from below.

George sighed, and Kelsi faced him. She figured the stunned, hollow look in his eyes meant he hadn't gotten much sleep.

"Where have you been?" she asked him finally. "Beth told us you came on Thursday . . ."

"Crashing in a motel in town," he mumbled. "It's pretty gross, but anything beats being . . . here. I'm going back to Boston later in the week. I got extra time off."

"Are you okay?" Kelsi couldn't help but ask.

"I don't know," George said. His legs hung over the ledge, dangling toward the shore below. "I don't think so. No, in fact, no."

Kelsi stared off across the water, remembering that rainy night she had been through about a year ago. Two soaking-wet people holding hands, walking across a parking lot. She remembered the breathless, desperate feeling. And all the tears.

"I know how you feel," she told George. "I don't know if it helps, but I've been there, too."

"Yeah," George said. "Beth left me this long, rambling message on my voice mail after . . . She mentioned you were dating him. I can't believe she would do this to both of us."

Kelsi was startled. Funny how, despite needling Beth about it earlier, she didn't feel bad about the fact that Adam was supposed to be dating her, not Beth.

"I meant last summer," she said. "And another guy. I went out with Adam a couple of times, but it wasn't a big deal. I just mean, you know, my feelings aren't hurt, too, that's all."

"I guess that's good," George said.

Kelsi nodded. She had never been that excited about Adam to begin with, if she thought about it. *Nice* really *wasn't* enough. Chemistry was so undefinable, so random. But it was everything. Kelsi thought briefly of Tim, then brushed the thought away.

"So that guy last summer," George said. "What happened?"

"He cheated on me," Kelsi said softly. "It sucked. I cried a lot. But it's not like you and Beth. He was just a . . . summer boy."

"But I bet the girl he cheated with wasn't some perfect lifeguard who rescued him," George added bitterly. "Some, like, beach god."

"Well, no," Kelsi said. "He cheated on me with Ella."

George's mouth opened in shock, and then he shut it with an audible snap.

"Um," he said.

"Yeah," Kelsi agreed.

George shuddered, and then, surprising both of them, he laughed. "I guess you win," he said. "Um . . . congratulations on the being the most screwed-over?"

"Thanks," Kelsi said drily.

"So tell me how you got past it," George said, looking closely at Kelsi. He seemed so vulnerable. "You've moved on, right?"

"I guess," Kelsi said, and Tim flashed into her head again. The way he'd looked at her that first night at the bonfire, and the way he'd hijacked her phone at the bowling alley. How much she laughed whenever he was around. She frowned slightly. Of course she hadn't been that into Adam. She'd already met Tim.

Tim wasn't anything like Peter, or any of the other guys Kelsi had lumped him with. In fact, she'd never met anyone like him before. She remembered what he'd said before the road trip: *It'll be great. I'll be great.*

It all sank in. Tim had done exactly what he'd said he would do on the road trip. He hadn't been flirting with Ella, he'd been preventing a catfight on I-95.

And she'd sent him away.

Kelsi felt her heart sink. Literally. All the way from her chest to her bare feet.

George sighed, sounding as dejected as Kelsi felt. "Beth wants to talk, and I don't even know what to talk about. I don't know where to start."

Kelsi tried to shrug off the horrible way she felt about Tim, and focus back on George. "She loves you," Kelsi told George, returning her attention to their conversation. She didn't know if that would help or hurt him at this point, but she felt compelled to say it anyway. "It might be hard to believe right now, but she does."

"I've loved her for so long," George said, quietly. "I'm pissed at her, but at the same time I don't know how to not be in love with her."

"I think you have to talk to her," Kelsi said. "Tell her exactly what you feel."

George was silent as he tugged some grass free of the earth beneath him. He ripped the blades into tiny pieces and scattered them into the wind. He didn't say a word, but Kelsi knew what he was feeling.

Suddenly, she missed Tim — and missed him even more when she realized she was unlikely to see him again, thanks entirely to her evil behavior. Kelsi had spent the summer focusing on how wrong he was for her. And now it seemed all too clear to her that she didn't want anyone *but* him. Not Peter. Not Adam. Just Tim.

Although Kelsi had wanted the cove all to herself, now she was glad George was there, even if it was just to keep her company while she mourned her lost opportunities. When George took her hand and held it tightly, she prayed that, in the end, they'd both get what they wanted.

Beth was pretty sure she had *feeling horrible* down to a science. And she didn't feel any better when George mysteriously turned up at the cottage late on Sunday afternoon.

Beth walked into the living room to find him watching a movie, his arms crossed over his chest. Her heart leaped. It was the first time she'd seen him since that awful night.

She looked at him for a moment and took in his dark tangle of hair and his arms, which were more muscular than she'd remembered, no doubt because of his summer spent painting. She glanced at his mouth and the nape of his neck — everything so wonderfully familiar — and she felt a deep emptiness inside.

"Hey," she said, clearing her throat.

George stared at her and said nothing. The longer he glared at her the larger the emptiness grew. Finally, George turned his attention back to the TV.

"Okay," Beth said after a long moment of silence. "I get that you, like, hate me now. But I'm glad you came back here anyway. We need to —"

George looked up at her again, and his eyes were so vacant that she immediately stopped talking.

"I can't afford the motel in town," he told her, his voice cold and foreign. "Your parents said it was cool if I stayed here."

"George, I'm so —" Beth whispered, feeling any resolve weaken.

George shook his head. "I came up this weekend to surprise you," he said slowly, each word like a sucker punch. "Which obviously worked beyond my wildest dreams. Huh?"

"Let's talk about this," Beth said desperately, relieved that he was talking to her at all.

"What should we talk about?" he demanded. "Tell me it was my imagination, Beth. Tell me I didn't see you with some other guy. Were you with him before? Did you hook up with him?"

"George . . ." she whispered, but she didn't know what else to say. Saying his name seemed to answer everything. *Yes, I cheated on you. Yes, I kissed another boy. A lot.*

"That's what I thought," George grunted. "I can't see you anymore, Beth. My friend went to camp up in Acadia. When he comes back this way tomorrow, I'm outta here."

Beth felt her lips trembling. George's jaw tightened, and he turned back to the movie. Beth bowed her head, wrapped her arms around herself, and then dashed out of the house.

The next day, when Adam called again, Beth decided to meet him in town after dinner that evening. Maybe, by talking to *him*, she'd be able to make some sense of the whole mess.

He was waiting outside the Twin Freeze, and when he saw her coming, he pulled himself upright and smiled.

"Beth! Hey!" Adam seemed so excited to see her that Beth smiled wider than she'd meant to. Maybe she was becoming one of those girly girls who practically faded away without a guy's attention. She had never thought of herself that way, but who knew? This summer she was a different person.

"Hey," she said back, and then they stood there for a lingering moment. Beth studied him and realized that, normally, she would have assumed a guy like Adam would never give her the time of day. He was too hot in an obvious way. But, ironically enough, being with George had given her the confidence to befriend Adam. To flirt with him. And more.

"How are you doing?" he asked.

Beth shrugged. "I've been better."

"Is he . . . Is it bad?"

Beth stared at him. "Um, yeah. It's bad."

"So he's still around?"

Beth shook her head. "You know, I can't really talk about George with you, okay?"

"Uh, okay. What should we talk about then?" Adam moved away from her.

"Well . . . uh . . ." Beth cast around for something to say, completely weirded out by the fact that only a week ago she couldn't seem to say *enough* to this guy, and now they couldn't have a simple conversation. "Maybe this is a mistake," she said. "Maybe I should just, um, go home —"

"No!" Adam said, putting out his hands to prevent her from leaving. "I mean, please don't. Come with me for a while. We'll just hang out, talk. It'll be fine. I promise."

And Beth really, really wanted *something* to be fine. So it seemed like the best thing to do was simply follow him.

"One for *Some Kind of Wonderful,* please," Ella said, smiling brightly at the girl behind the glass at the Royale movie theater.

Kelsi had told Ella to be subtle with Jeremy because he clearly was the type of guy who wanted to get to know a girl before he got physical with her. Which, up until Ella had met Jeremy, she hadn't thought possible.

But then Ella had realized that Jeremy was the good guy she'd been looking for all along. So, the night after her return from Amherst, she decided to seek him out, and show him just how subtle she could be.

Ella bought herself some popcorn and a soda, and checked herself out in one of the gilded mirrors that lined the once-plush walls. Not exactly her usual boy-magnet attire. Tonight she wore her oldest pair of jeans and a yellow T-shirt from the Gap. Granted, the jeans clung to her curves and she'd shrunk the tee so it barely covered her midriff, but the fact remained: She was wearing jeans and a T-shirt.

The point here was to impress the guy with her personality and not just her body, Ella reminded herself.

This was truly revolutionary.

Ella pushed her way through the theater's double doors and started scanning the aisles. There weren't too many people at an eleven o'clock screening of an old movie, but there were more than Ella had imagined there would be.

And there, near the front, was the one person Ella had been counting on.

From afar, she admired his shaggy dark hair and the casual way he slouched in his seat. She felt something tug at her heart as she made her way toward him, and it wasn't just nerves.

Taking a breath, Ella fixed a smile on her face and helped herself to the aisle seat he'd left open next to him.

"This seat isn't taken, is it?" she asked sweetly, enjoying the look of shock on Jeremy's face.

"Ella!" His dark eyes went wide and curious. "What are you doing here?"

"What does it look like?" she asked. She put her soda in the drink holder and relaxed back in her seat.

"Um." Jeremy kept staring at her. "Do you actually like this movie?" he asked.

Ella tossed a kernel of popcorn into her mouth and chewed it for a moment, thoughtfully. "I don't know," she said. "I don't think I've seen it."

He was frowning when she looked at him, so she smiled her full-wattage smile, because even if he was looking at her like she was crazy, she was just so happy to be near him again.

"Well," he said, his face brightening. "You're in for a treat."

"I certainly hope so," Ella said.

And she got to see him smile at her again, just as the lights went down.

After the movie, Ella and Jeremy walked down along the main street of Pebble Beach under the heavy August moonlight.

So far, Ella had to admit, the evening had been pretty much perfect. She and Jeremy had discussed and debated the film — Ella thought the ending was predictable, but Jeremy found it flawless. And not once had Ella tried to put the moves on him. So Kelsi might just know what she was talking about, after all. Ella still wasn't sure what had inspired Kelsi to forgive her, much less start dispensing romantic advice. But Ella just felt lucky to have a sister like Kelsi.

In fact, being with Jeremy, Ella felt lucky all around. She wasn't sure she deserved it, so she just tried to keep feeling grateful.

She was amazed to discover just how much fun it was to *talk* to a guy she also thought was hot. It was like a whole different dimension, she realized as they strolled along and Jeremy explained his film obsession.

"Life just isn't edited enough," he said with a wide grin. "In the movies, the camera always blacks out at the best moment. How boring would it be to watch, like, all those dull moments where people were daydreaming and staring off into space?"

"You only like the good parts," Ella clarified. She could relate.

"I like to watch them," Jeremy said, nodding. "Maybe someday I'll head out to Hollywood and make movies myself. Why not, right? It's the American dream." He turned slightly, so he was glancing at Ella as they ambled along. "What about you? What's your dream?"

"Me?" Ella was taken aback. With any other guy, she would have said something leading and teasing, like, *You're my dream, baby*. But with Jeremy, she knew he didn't want a line. He really wanted to know. And more to the point, Ella didn't want to play games with him anymore. She just wanted to . . . *be*.

"Everyone has a dream," Jeremy added, still smiling at her.

"Well, I've always thought I'd be good at fashion," Ella said. "I like clothes, and how they go together."

"You mean, like being a model?"

"Please." Ella wrinkled her nose at him. "I'm, like, three feet tall. I couldn't be a model."

"I don't know," Jeremy said. "I think the only problem would be the height thing. Everything else, you've got."

Ella liked the warm glow that his compliment gave her, but she didn't latch onto it. She wanted to finish her earlier thought.

"I'd really like to, I don't know, design stuff," she said. "Clothes or bags. Maybe shoes." She looked down at the pair of jeans she'd rolled up at the cuffs to accentuate the pair of sandals she wore. It was a small alteration, sure, but she always did something creative with her outfits. Kelsi always commented that a T-shirt on Ella was an entirely different garment than the same T-shirt on her.

"That's really cool," Jeremy said. "You should think about it."

They made their way down to the end of the pier and stood there, leaning against the rail and watching the sea. There was a bonfire farther down the beach, but Ella had no desire to be there.

"I'm glad you wanted to see me again," Jeremy said after a long moment of comfortable silence. Ella looked up at him, inquiringly. "You know, after last time."

Ella cringed at the memory. "I think I got carried away."

Ugh, she thought. *Awkward much?*

"See, here's the thing," Jeremy said, looking her full in the face and, for once, not seeming shy. "You know that you could have any guy you wanted, right?"

"I don't want just any guy," Ella said, without the flirty inflection she might normally use.

"And it's not that I don't want . . ." He stopped, and shook his head. "I want to get to know you. The real you. So that anything that happens between us can also be . . . real." His eyes searched hers. "Do you know what I mean?"

Ella thought about all the boys she'd known in her life, all the boys who'd fallen for her, kissed her, pursued her, and who, when she really thought about it, had known nothing about her. Jeremy already knew more than all those past boys combined. She'd never told anyone about her dreams before. No boy had ever asked.

Except for the one by her side.

She looked up at Jeremy and smiled.

"I know exactly what you mean," she said.

He smiled back, and then he did something totally unexpected. He leaned in close, and kissed her.

It was such a sweet kiss. Only lips, and that was more than enough to get Ella heated up. When he pulled away, they were both grinning from ear to ear, and Jeremy slid his hand over hers, and held it softly.

It's distinctly possible, Ella realized through the swell of happiness, *that I may have found myself a nice guy after all.*

And it sure didn't hurt that, behind that shaggy hair, he was absolutely beautiful.

32

"I've been thinking a lot about what happened," Adam told Beth as soon as they found a place to stand in the crowd. The restaurant part of Ahoy was just as packed as the bar, which was only to be expected in midsummer. Pebble Beach would be a mob scene for the rest of August, and then turn quiet right after Labor Day.

"So have I," Beth replied. *You have no idea.*

"And even though I know it's been really tough on you — and I wish I could change that — maybe what happened was for the best." His eyes were hopeful.

"For the best?" she echoed incredulously. "Adam, everything has basically gone to hell."

"I don't mean . . ." Adam looked down. "I just think that maybe things sometimes turn out the way they're supposed to. Maybe your boyfriend stumbling in on us like that was just a really brutal way —"

"Adam, please don't," Beth said, cutting him off. "I can't . . . I mean, I really don't know why I even came out tonight."

"To give yourself a break," Adam said softly. "I know you're upset, Beth, and I hate seeing you like this."

"Thanks," Beth told him. "I could use a friend right now." She bit her lip.

"Beth, listen," he said in a low, urgent voice. "I want to be your friend. But you know how strong my feelings are, don't you? I think we could be so much more than friends. If we let ourselves."

Beth was about to remind Adam that they *had* let themselves, but then something awful happened.

A huge crowd pushed past them and they had to take a few steps around a nearby table. Beth staggered back and bumped into a booth, where George was sharing a plate of fries with Kelsi.

Time stopped.

Kelsi appeared horrified. George looked frozen.

Beth could only imagine the stunned expression she had on her face. "Oh, no," she whispered.

"Gee, this is awkward," George said loudly, his eyes on Beth's face.

"We just came here to talk," Beth tried to explain, gesturing to Adam.

"Sure," George said. "Talking. Sex. Same difference."

"You don't have to listen to this," Adam told Beth, putting his hand on her arm. "I told you this was all for the best." He began to lead Beth away.

George's expression changed. "You should probably take your hands off my girlfriend," he said to Adam, slowly getting to his feet.

"Or what?" Adam shot back. He paused for a moment, and Beth could see that he welcomed this confrontation. "You want to take a swing at me, go right ahead."

Girlfriend, Beth realized, and she felt a surge of hope. George had called her his girlfriend, despite everything.

"Yeah, whatever," George said, sliding to one side of the booth.

"What, you're not man enough?" Adam challenged.

"You tell me," George said, stepping closer.

"Both of you, stop!" Beth cried, hurrying to stand between them.

George turned his attention to Beth then, and she almost crumbled when she saw how fiery his eyes were.

"George —"

"You were right. He's really cool, Bethy," he told her in a low voice. "Enjoy each other, okay?" Then he turned and walked off into the crowd.

"I'm sorry, Beth," Kelsi said, clambering out of the booth.

Beth was too disoriented to respond. But she noticed how Adam threw himself down into the booth the moment it was vacated. He was literally trying to take George's place.

"I'm gonna go to the bonfire on the beach," Kelsi said, giving Beth's arm a gentle squeeze. "See you there?"

Beth managed to shrug. Once Kelsi wandered off, Beth put

a hand on her stomach, hoping to settle it down. Then she looked at Adam.

"Take a seat," he urged her. "We came here to talk, remember?"

"I don't want to talk," Beth said, her voice steady at last.

Suddenly, she was noticing that Adam really did resemble George. It was the way he tilted his head when he talked. But he didn't have an ounce of George's funny, genuine vibe. How could she have *ever* wanted to choose between the two of them?

It made sense. Beth had missed George so much, she'd practically been drowning. So she'd grabbed on to Adam, like he was a life raft.

Adam may have saved her life. But without George, her life was meaningless. *I am George's girlfriend,* she realized. *What am I even doing with this other guy?*

"I have to go," Beth said abruptly.

"What?" Adam looked startled. "You're not going after him, are you?"

"Damn right I am," she said confidently. She hadn't felt this strong in a long time.

"Beth . . ." Adam seemed to be at a loss. "Don't do this."

"I'm sorry, Adam," Beth said softly. "I'm in love with George. I always have been."

"Wait a minute," Adam pleaded.

"I have to go," Beth said again, very firmly. She felt awful for hurting Adam's feelings, but every second she stood there with him was one second she was losing with George. She said good-bye again, then started pushing her way through the crowd.

When Beth made it outside, she breathed in the cool night air. Her course seemed completely clear for the first time all summer.

She'd do anything it took to get George back.

"The thing is, Beth," George said coolly. "I just don't think this will work out. Okay?"

Beth had caught up with him down near the beach. He'd been for a long walk, he told her. Communing with the rocks and the dunes.

Which pretty much translated to, *Avoiding you, Beth, the person who took a chain saw to my heart.*

"I can't blame you for feeling like that," Beth said. "I messed up. Big-time. It was a huge mistake."

George just raised his eyebrows at her, not disputing her choice of words.

"So I don't expect anything from you," Beth continued. "But I just want you to give me one last chance."

He studied her carefully. Even though she almost always knew what George was thinking, now she couldn't imagine what was going through his mind.

"You left him?" he asked. "Back at Ahoy?"

Beth nodded. "I went with him on a whim tonight, George. It meant nothing. I promise you." She took a deep breath and added, "And nothing else I did with him *ever* meant anything. I want you to know that. Yes, we kissed and fooled around once. But I *didn't* sleep with him, George. I never would have." She swallowed hard.

George furrowed his brow. "Part of me believes you, Bethy. But I don't know how to . . . get past it all."

Beth felt relief flood through her. "Will you let me show you?"

"How?"

"Come on," Beth said, and reached over to grab his hand before she talked herself out of it. "Follow me."

"Do you recognize this?" she asked a few silent minutes later, standing on the beach about midway between the water-line and the beach grass.

"Um, sand?" George asked.

"Last summer, you left your clothes in a big heap right here, while you were skinny-dipping with that girl."

George stared at the ground, so Beth knew he remembered.

"*I* stole them," Beth said, and tugged on his arm to pull him after her.

He followed, still not saying anything, and she led him across the sand and onto the street. There was a streetlight casting a perfect circle on the ground, and Beth pointed at it.

"I put them here."

"Just to be clear," George said, and Beth was so happy to hear the familiar jokey lilt to his voice. "You're actually *admitting* you stole my clothes? After an entire year of claiming it must have been a passing vagrant who did it?"

It was the most encouraging thing she'd heard from him yet, but Beth hid her relieved smile.

She walked a little bit farther up the road to stand outside a green split-level house. Everything around them seemed deserted, because everyone in town was attending the bonfire.

"And this is the house you climbed on, completely naked, to yell at me," she said. "I would climb up myself, to set the mood, but I'm kind of afraid I'd break my neck." She laughed nervously. "Also, you know, I hate heights."

George looked up at the roof, and then down to the end of the road, where it ended right before the woods.

"What are we doing?" he asked quietly.

Beth swallowed, hard. "I wanted to show you that I remember," she whispered.

"That you remember what?"

"Last summer. Us." Beth felt something lodge in her throat, tighter than before, and swallowed again, even harder. "I want to show you that I remember everything. Every little detail. No matter how . . . lost I got while you were away."

George remained silent. Beth wished she could see his face, but it was dark and there were too many shadows.

"I don't think I can do this," he said.

"I'm not done yet!" Beth was desperate, and she could hear it in her own high-pitched voice, which had reached cartoon character levels. "It was right here, in this very spot, that I realized that I was in love with you — did you know that? And then later, we had our first kiss —"

"I remember, Beth," George said. "I never needed reminding."

That was all Beth needed to hear. Suddenly, she felt reckless.

And inspired.

"Stay here," she ordered him.

Beth turned and headed through the backyard, to the rear of the house. She eyed the lattice that stretched from the ground up to the roof, and steeled herself. She was determined. Her fear of heights would just have to go away . . . right . . . now.

She began to climb — hand over hand, concentrating on the next hold and never looking down. Soon enough, she was pulling herself onto the rooftop. Her heart was banging against her chest and her breath was coming fast and shallow, like she'd just gone for a run. But she felt exhilarated.

Beth scooted across the roof on her butt, and peered over the side. George was still standing there, gazing at the ground, lost in thought.

"George!" she yelled.

He looked around, and then turned in a circle, still not seeing her.

"What the hell are you doing?" he called, sounding annoyed. "Come back here and . . ." His words trailed off as he glanced up, and gaped at her.

"Check me out!" Beth said, and waved.

"Beth, this isn't funny," he said nervously. "You're going to hurt yourself, because if you fall, I can guarantee I'm not going to catch you."

Beth saw she had no choice but to stand up and start shouting.

"I LOVE YOU, GEORGE!" she screamed into the night. "I LOVE *YOU*, GEORGE!"

"Beth!" he hissed.

For a second she thought about stopping, but Beth could hear that George wasn't as pissed as he was pretending to be.

So she got louder.

"I'M SORRY, GEORGE!" she bellowed, waving her arms around. She had to close her eyes because she couldn't look at the ground too much. "I'M SO SORRY! I LOVE YOU! BETH TUTTLE LOVES —"

"Okay!" he shouted back, and he was definitely laughing now. Lights went on a bit farther down the block. "I get it. Just come down."

"I can't," Beth said.

"Uh, why not?"

"I'm afraid of heights," Beth explained. "I'm pretty much stuck here."

He looked up at her for a long time.

"Wow, living on a roof is going to be tough. Just think about what you'll have to do if you need to use the bathroom."

"George!"

"Okay," he said finally. "I'm coming up."

George made his way toward the lattice, and for the first time since Thursday night, Beth had an inkling that everything might just work out, after all.

After Kelsi left the insanity at Ahoy, she found herself down at the beach, wandering through the crowd around the bonfire. Kids milled around in packs while adults settled down in folding chairs, armed with martini shakers.

Kelsi looked around, trying to decide what she wanted to do. The summers always seemed to begin and end with a bonfire. Kelsi couldn't believe she would be headed to college in just a few short weeks. Would college change her? What new discoveries awaited her there? She was nervous, but she couldn't wait to find out.

When a group of younger kids jostled past her, Kelsi smiled and shook her head. She'd been in what Ella called her Philosophy Zone. Ella claimed that Kelsi always lived inside her head, and as a result, missed out on good stuff happening around her.

Sometimes her little sister had a point.

Since it was a chilly night, she found herself a spot near the fire. She was about to settle down on the sand when she noticed a familiar group just a few feet away. The same big orange cooler, the same frat boy types, and, most important, the same Tim, standing with them.

Okay. Kelsi knew now. She'd come to the bonfire tonight because she thought there was a really good chance Tim would be here, too. Deep down where all her rationality couldn't reach, Kelsi couldn't deny it anymore: She wanted to be with Tim.

She watched him, talking and laughing with his friends. She studied his golden hair and tan skin and slow, easy smile. He left her almost breathless.

Wow, Kelsi thought. *I've got it bad.*

Tim looked over then, and their eyes met. His face seemed to freeze, and then his eyes lit up. Then, his usual smirk kicked in. Kelsi had missed seeing that expression so much, she felt an intense heat that she knew had nothing to do with the roaring fire. Tim raised his can of beer in a wordless toast.

Kelsi felt paralyzed for a minute. Her mind was racing.

And then Kelsi thought of Ella again and realized that this was no time to live in her head.

There was a time for subtlety, as Kelsi had taught Ella, and then there was a time for action.

Without a moment of hesitation, Kelsi crossed the distance between them.

Tim looked surprised, then wary as she drew closer. Kelsi

realized with a rush of relief that Tim didn't look upset with her at all. He'd gotten past their fight. Maybe, as Ella had said, boys *could* put up with a lot.

Kelsi came to a stop in front of Tim and looked up, soaking in his nearness and the sheer *rightness* of this guy.

Then she reached up, took hold of his jaw with one hand, and kissed him.

No words. Just her mouth across his.

Tim was still for a heartbeat, and then he kissed her back, his arms going around her waist to pull her in tight against him.

Even better than expected, Kelsi thought, enjoying the warmth and pressure of his mouth against hers.

And then she stopped all that thinking completely.

"Just follow my hands," George said in Beth's ear. "You don't have to look. Just close your eyes and feel."

They were stuck midway down the lattice. George was directly behind her, their bodies pressed close in a way that Beth would have loved if she hadn't been paralyzed with fear.

"I'm trying," she whispered. But she was holding on so tight, the wood was cutting into her palms, and she wasn't sure she was still breathing.

"Come on, Bethy," George said. "You know I won't let anything happen to you."

Beth squeezed her eyes shut, pried her hand from the lattice, and let George guide her down.

When they reached the ground, Beth actually rolled over onto her stomach and kissed the pavement.

"You were fine," George told her. "Except maybe for that middle part. I thought we might have to stay there overnight."

"Overnight?" Beth waved a dismissive hand. "I was think-ing forever, like garden gnomes."

"We're too cute to be gnomes," George said, and laughed.

Beth laughed, too, and climbed to her feet. She could feel George's iciness dissolving.

"We should probably get out of here before someone calls the cops, like last year," she said, heading for the street.

"You're just jealous because my performance drew the cops down here, while yours was so uninspiring that no one bothered to call them," George was chiding her again, just like it was any other day.

Beth thought he looked perfect, laughing in the dark under the streetlights. But then his laughter slowed a little bit as he looked at her, and his bright eyes started to darken.

"I said I would do anything for you," Beth said, refusing to break eye contact. "Didn't I?"

"Beth, I love you," George told her, his voice husky. "I just don't know . . . I can't stop thinking about you and Adam together. Maybe it's a guy thing." He stopped, and shook his head. "I'm sorry, Bethy. I've thought about it and thought about it, and I just go in circles."

"I wish I hadn't fooled around with Adam more than I'll ever be able to tell you. I know I can't change what happened but . . ." She trailed off, trying to find the right words.

George nodded sullenly.

"I'm so sorry," she said again, and then she stepped for-ward and hugged him.

Beth wrapped her arms around George's back and nestled

into his neck the way she usually did, when there was no distance between them. George made a small sound, and his body tensed, but then he started to relax. His arms crept around to hold her, and then he was pulling her close, and dropping his head down beside hers. Beth felt warmth on her face and realized she was crying — and he was, too.

"It was always about you," Beth whispered. "I know that sounds crazy, but it's true. It was because I missed you so much I —"

"Beth," George whispered, stroking her hair. "I understand."

"Thanks for saying that."

"I can't be without you," George said simply. "I just can't."

"You don't have to be," she promised him, and held him tight, as if she'd never let go.

Later, they walked back toward the cottages, holding hands, talking quietly, filling each other in on their separate summers.

George talked about his job, relaying crazy stories about stupid adventures at MIT. Beth bragged about her surfing prowess, claiming she put the cast of *Blue Crush* to shame, and George would be stunned by how great she'd gotten. George said she'd have to show him tomorrow, before he left.

When they got back to the cottage, it was dark.

"Everyone must still be at the bonfire," Beth said, glancing around.

When she looked at George, his eyes had changed, or

deepened somehow. Beth felt her breath catch as if she were back up on the roof.

He didn't say anything. Beth felt emotion swell inside her like an enormous wave that she wanted to ride until it crashed upon the shore. Wordlessly, they drew close to each other, and then George took her by the hand and pulled her up the stairs, down the corridor into his room.

George closed the door, and they faced each other. Beth realized she was holding her breath. Everything — all their earlier tension, Adam, the fight, the tears — seemed to disappear in that one instant. All Beth saw and felt was George. As he came closer to her, she reached up and traced his mouth with her finger. Their being together felt so inevitable. So right.

Beth realized that she had been waiting for this moment all summer. If not all her life.

George ran his finger along the side of her face, and swallowed hard. "Bethy," he murmured, "I love you so much."

Beth wanted to respond in kind, but found she could barely speak. She let herself fall into George's arms.

He kissed her, softly, cupping her face in his warm hands as he so often did. Beth sighed into his mouth, thrilling at the feel of his lips on hers. To think she had feared she might never enjoy a delicious George kiss again. The kiss intensified and deepened, and their arms went around each other. Beth could feel how much George wanted her. How much they both wanted . . . *this.*

Still kissing, they walked backward to the bed, and

collapsed together in a tangle of limbs. *Oh, George.* Only he could make her quiver this way.

Beth noticed her hands were trembling when she peeled off George's T-shirt. Beth couldn't help but grin when she saw what a summer's worth of labor had done to his body. George might never be tan, but he was definitely buff.

"Wow," she whispered, staring.

"You like?" George asked with a grin, flexing his left arm.

Beth giggled, reaching over and squeezing his impressive bicep. "Not half bad."

This was exactly why she was so in love with George, Beth realized, as she rested her head on his bare chest, and he cradled her in his arms. They could swing from tender to silly and back again in a heartbeat.

"Are you thinking what I'm thinking?" George murmured, reaching down to gently slide Beth's tank top over her head.

Beth nuzzled his neck, savoring the sensation of her bare skin against his. Then, she drew back and studied George. "You mean, that this is . . ."

"The Moment." George nodded, a huge smile creeping over his face.

"Great minds think alike," Beth said, wrapping her arms around his neck.

"Are we ready?" George whispered.

"I am if you are," Beth answered, her voice steady and her eyes on his. Deliberately, she reached down and unbuttoned his cargo shorts.

"No candles in the vicinity. Condoms waiting in my wallet. And no parents." George grinned, stroking Beth's bare back in slow, teasing circles. "I think we're okay."

Slowly, carefully they undressed each other. Beth realized they were both shaking a little, and kept grinning at each other, equally nervous and excited.

"We can still wait if you want," George whispered, drawing her close to kiss her again.

"I don't want to wait another second," Beth murmured.

And so they didn't.

Much later, they dressed and snuck outside to lie in the hammock and wait for morning. The others had come back from the bonfire, but were all sleeping by then.

"It's a tradition," George said, yawning as they cuddled close in the wide hammock.

Beth buried her face in his chest and smiled. She never wanted to leave the safe circle of his arms.

When she heard his breathing change, she glanced up and saw he was sleeping, his lashes resting on his cheeks, and his chest rising and falling. She admired him for a long minute, then rolled over and looked up at the sky. It was the darkest hour — right before dawn — and Beth noticed how the sky was full of stars. She remembered how she'd thought the night looked messy with stars that first evening at Pebble Beach. It had almost been an omen, then. This summer *had* been messy in so many ways.

But now, cuddled close to George, everything seemed to be back in order again. Beth was right where she should have been all along.

Soon, dawn started to creep in. The birds chattered and the dew clung to the grass. Frost would be coming soon, and after that, autumn.

Beth felt wonderfully tired, but she wanted to bask in every last second of this summer. So she kept herself awake and held George close, watching as the world finally brightened all around them.

Take a sneak peek at this summer's hottest beach read:

POOL BOYS

BY ERIN HAFT

Turn the page and dive right in . . .

The Silver Oaks Country Club
~ A FAMILY INSTITUTION ~

Rules:

Members will treat fellow members with respect and decorum.

Members will not engage socially with staff.

Members will not smoke on the premises.

Members will leave their pets at home.

Members will not gamble or place any unapproved wagers while on the premises.

Members will wear approved footgear at all times in the dining room.

UNSPOKEN RULES: (By Brooke, Charlotte, and Georgia)

1. Never Underestimate an Entrance.

2. Thou Shalt not Poach Thy Friend's Love Interest.

3. Sportsmanship, Schmortsmanship...

4. In Case of Rain, Please Convene in the Billiards Room to Watch the Pool Boys Make Jackasses of Themselves, Trying to Play "Pool."

5. I forget.

6. Don't Toss Out Anything of Value. Also Stay Away from the Cabana After Certain People Have Used It.

Chapter One

The First Unspoken Rule

"You guys?" Brooke Farnsworth whispered to her two best friends. "I've seen the future, and his name is Marcus Craft. I told you this summer would be killer, didn't I?"

Brooke huddled with Georgia Palmer and Charlotte von Klaus in the shadows of the cabana entrance, surveying the otherwise deserted pool patio in the bright June morning. There was still a chill in the air — in coastal Connecticut, summer never truly kicked in until July — and she shivered, partly from the breeze, and partly from delight.

Brooke glanced back inside at the terry-cloth robes hanging near the door, freshly washed and waiting, the silver *S O* monograms glinting on each lapel. (Every item of white cloth on the premises of the Silver Oaks Country Club bore the same stitched silver monogram, from the napkins in the dining room to the curtains in the parlor.) Maybe she and Georgia and Charlotte should have worn robes over their bikinis? Nah. . . .

Brooke turned back toward the pool. It was all just as she remembered from last June: the piles of fluffy towels, the empty loungers, the water like a solid block of blue ice.

Everything that symbolized the start of another typical Silver Oaks season . . . everything that is, except for the shaggy blond boy in the lifeguard chair.

"I thought you said this summer would be more of the same old, same old," Georgia teased.

"Did I?" Brooke whispered back. "Please stop listening to anything I say at school."

"Let's just hope he can swim," Charlotte muttered.

The three girls broke into laughter, but Brooke quickly brought a hand to her glossy lips. She didn't want Marcus Craft to notice her. Not quite yet. She wanted him to spy her as she strolled over and settled into her usual lounger at the far edge of the patio, the one under the big green umbrella, right next to the ivy-covered fence adjoining the tennis courts. Brooke had been settling into that lounger for as long as she'd been wearing a bikini, and she'd learned how to play it for its full effect.

Brooke was obsessed with entrances.

"Is he looking at me?" Brooke whispered. She brushed a lone strand of shiny black hair out of her hazel eyes, then pulled a tube of sunblock out of her fringed Botkia bag, squeezing a dollop of cream on her shoulders. Thankfully Marcus was too far away to read the 45 SPF label.

Charlotte snickered.

"What?" Brooke said.

"Yes, he's looking at you," Georgia groaned. "Who else would he look at?"

"Sweetie, you're the one who's tall, blonde, and gorgeous." Brooke raised her eyebrows at Georgia over her new Marc Jacobs sunglasses. (Props to Mom for the shades: In spite of the woman's fiendishness, Theresa Farnsworth always came through with the perfect end-of-school-year present.) "And, as far as males are concerned, tall, blond, and gorgeous trumps short, black-haired, and pale every day of the week."

"You're *raven*-haired," Charlotte chided. "You have to remember that, B. You're not pale; you're porcelain. You're not short; you're petite. Just like I'm *not* an Orphan Annie clone." Charlotte flipped her long red curls over her shoulder and struck an exaggeratedly seductive pose. "I'm a fiery she-demon. Have I taught you nothing?"

"You did once, I think," Brooke said dryly. She tucked the sunblock back in her bag. "You taught me how to pad my bra. In the cabana, the summer after seventh grade."

"I think you taught me that, too," Georgia told Charlotte.

"I think I taught me that, three," Charlotte added.

They laughed again, and Brooke glanced toward the lifeguard chair. Remarkably, Marcus *was* looking at her. She felt a tingle of anticipation.

"Hey, Marcus!" Charlotte called suddenly, stepping into the sunshine and waving up to him, high on his lonely perch over the center of the pool. "It's Marcus, isn't it? I'm Charlotte, and this is Brooke and Georgia. We know everything there is to know about Silver Oaks — especially the bad stuff. So if you have any questions — you know, questions about things you don't want to ask anyone else — feel free to ask us."

And thank you, C, for stealing my entrance, Brooke thought with a smirk.

"Uh . . . okay," Marcus called back. He flashed a puzzled grin, his blue eyes roving over the three of them. Clearly, he had no idea what Charlotte was talking about. But then, few people other than Georgia or Brooke *ever* knew what Charlotte von Klaus was talking about. "Thanks. Nice to meet you."

"The pleasure's all ours," Charlotte replied under her breath.

Brooke suppressed a smile as she trailed Charlotte and Georgia across the flagstones toward the opposite side of the pool, their flip-flops slapping in an uneven rhythm. She couldn't help but steal another peek at the lifeguard as she grabbed a towel. Marcus's presence was a sign. Definitely. How could it not be? It wasn't just that she and Charlotte and Georgia were the first to arrive at the pool — per tradition, of course — on the first day of the new season, and therefore the first to spot this new boy. It wasn't even that he was ridiculously hot, with the square jaw, the blond mane, and the cocoa tan. . . .

It was that he was new.

The last handsome new employee at Silver Oaks had been Ethan Brennan, the twenty-year-old tennis instructor. And that had been two years ago. Plus, Ethan wasn't hot; he was cute (there *is* a difference) in a sort of crunchy slacker way. And, as a junior at the local community college, he also seemed content to spend the rest of his life at Silver Oaks. Which was fine. But it meant that thirty years from now, he'd still be giving tennis lessons and roaming the grounds making wisecracks, while Brooke, Georgia, and Charlotte discussed their kids' outrageous college tuition.

Not that Brooke would ever have said any of this out loud. Georgia had briefly dated Ethan last summer, in a rare and direct violation of the Spoken Rules. Worse, Brooke knew Georgia was still wrestling with some lingering feelings for him. But that was a whole other can of worms, and one not worth opening. Ethan Brennan was old news. Brooke could already tell that Marcus was different. How perfect was it that he was a lifeguard? With white sunscreen on his nose, no less! They used to make cheesy *movies* about lifeguards with white sunscreen. One rainy afternoon last summer, after a few G&Ts, Mrs. Farnsworth had forced Brooke and Georgia and Charlotte to watch a "Beach Blanket" movie marathon, starring some horrible-haired guy named Frankie Avalon. (The pastel bathing suits were classic, though. Why were older generations so afraid of skin?) A romance with a new lifeguard was a tradition. Or, rather, it *should* have been at a country club like Silver Oaks. Brooke practically owed it to herself to try it out.

"I can't *believe* I said this summer was going to be more of the same old, same old," she murmured. She kicked off her flip-flops and stretched out her legs, sinking into the lounger's familiar white cushions — all the while pretending to be oblivious to the possibility that Marcus was still staring at her. "I am an idiot."

"Brooke, you shouldn't confess so much out in the open," a gravelly male voice announced.

She sat up and turned around. *Speak of the devil.* Ethan Brennan stood on the other side of the fence, his curly brown hair tousled. He clutched his racket in one hand, trying to clear away the ivy with the other. Not surprisingly, his Silver Oaks–issued tennis whites were just a little less pristine than the robes hanging in the cabana.

"Hey there, Mr. Tennis Pro," Brooke said. "I was just thinking about you."

"That's funny, I was just thinking about me, too," he replied with a lazy smile.

By the looks of his jawline, he hadn't shaved in several days. But that was Ethan. He wasn't trying to cultivate a scruffy image; he'd probably just forgotten. Fortunately for him, he was just sexy enough to get away with a rumpled uniform and scruff.

"Don't you know better than to listen in on ladies' conversations, Ethan?" Charlotte quipped, settling into the lounger beside Brooke.

Grinning, Ethan swatted a stray vine out his face and hung on the chain-link fence. "I can't help it. I get high on eavesdropping. And on trying to scrounge a decent tennis game before the dinosaurs arrive — oops! I mean your parents. G, what do you say to a quick set?"

"I . . . well, I'm in my bikini," Georgia stammered. She stood awkwardly, fiddling with her towel. "I have to change."

"Come on. It'll be fun. We haven't played in so long. Seriously. I'm desperate for a good game."

Georgia glanced at Brooke and Charlotte. The message in her anxious, dark-blue eyes was plain: *Please help make up an excuse for me, you guys. He still calls me "G." He still jokes around with me. It's still too weird, even after all this time.*

For reasons Brooke couldn't fathom, Ethan had insisted on remaining friends with Georgia after their breakup. Brooke knew that Georgia wanted to get over him and get on with her life. But there was one problem: She was too nice to blow him off. Literally. Brooke had known Georgia her whole life, and couldn't remember her friend saying a mean thing about anyone, *ever*. She'd been displeased with people, sure: her parents, Ethan, even Brooke and Charlotte every now and then ... but she's always kept her moods to herself. One day that girl was going to burst.

"We just got here, Ethan," Brooke piped up. "Besides, you won't have to wait long for a game. My mom is changing into her new tennis whites as we speak. She spent all of May shopping for the perfect outfit: a conservative version of Venus Williams's minidresses. You'll be proud. But the three of us have to catch up. You know, girl stuff."

He chuckled. "Girl stuff? You guys talk to each other every single day. You go to the same school, don't you?" His eyes drifted over to the pool. "Hey, have you met the new girl yet? She seems really cool."

"What new girl?" the three girls all asked at the same time.

Brooke turned. "Where . . . ?" Her voice trailed off.

A tall, cheap-looking blonde had appeared out of nowhere — in a black Versace bikini. *The exact same one Brooke was wearing.* And now she was standing in front of the lifeguard chair, shaking hands with Marcus Craft. And he was trying not to stare her chest. And . . . okay, she wasn't so cheap-looking. Far from it. She was Georgia's height, but skinnier — with flawless skin and a cascade of curls that rivaled Charlotte's. Except *her* curls were golden, like Cinderella's.

This was not good. Miss Thing had not only stolen Brooke's bathing suit (unintentionally, but still), but she'd made contact with the guy Brooke had spotted first. How had *that* happened? She didn't belong here. Not this early, on the first day of the season. This was Brooke and Georgia and Charlotte's time. *And look at how she's flirting,* Brooke fumed. She and Marcus Craft were already making chit-chat, like a couple of newly partnered models preparing for a *Vogue* ad. Obviously, the new girl, whoever she was, had figured out the First Unspoken Rule. And she'd made her entrance right under Brooke's nose.

". . . name is Valerie," Ethan was saying. "She just moved here from New York. Her parents are friends with the Millers, on Old Pond Road. I wonder if *she* plays tennis."

"Valerie, huh?" Charlotte mumbled. "She's pretty."

"She's really pretty," Georgia agreed, sounding depressed.

"Please," Brooke said dismissively, readjusting her shades. She settled back into the lounger with a sigh. "You're both a thousand times hotter."

"Ha!" Ethan laughed.

Brooke frowned. "What's so funny?"

"Nothing." He cleared his throat. "Sorry. That came out wrong. I just love how you three always stick up for each other. You're like a street gang." He gestured toward Brooke's left arm, then Charlotte's, then Georgia's. "That's why you still wear those ratty friendship bracelets, right? It's like your gang tattoo."

Brooke glanced down at the bracelet on her wrist. It was pretty ratty, the plaid pattern long faded. Maybe it *was* time to take the damn thing off. But she wasn't going to be the first to do it. In eighth grade, at a county fair, she, Charlotte, and Georgia had bought matching patterns on a goofy whim, mostly to poke fun at their own obsession with fashion.

"I thought you said we're like a trio of back-up singers," Georgia muttered blushing as she avoided Ethan's gaze.

"He came up with that line when he was in his 'special place.'" Charlotte brought her thumb and forefinger to her lips and puffed on an imaginary joint.

"How many times do I have to tell you?" Ethan protested. "I —"

"Don't smoke pot," Brooke cut in. She removed her sunglasses and lowered her voice. "But you don't really think the new girl is all that hot, do you, Brennan?"

"Well, I mean, she —" Ethan bit his full lower lip, his cheeks flushing slightly. "She actually said something about you, Brooke."

Brooke's eyes narrowed. "Why? She doesn't even know me."

"Yeah, I know, but . . ." A smile crept across his stubbly face.

"What?" Brooke pressed.

"She thinks *you're* hot," he said. "I mean, not like she's attracted to you or anything. And I know you hate when people say this . . ."

"What?"

"She said you look like Snow White," Ethan finished.

Georgia and Charlotte burst out laughing. Even Brooke had to smile. It was a classic, a perennial — all part of the never-ending, attempted Disneyfication of her life. Every single Silver Oaks member had tried to force the label on Brooke at one time or another. *How pretty you are! You look just like Snow White!* Maybe they figured if they said it enough, Brooke's life *would* become a G-rated fairy tale. Maybe that was what they expected from a girl whose father was president of the board of Silver Oaks.

Perfection.

Yeah, right.

"And when did Valerie have this amazing epiphany?" Brooke asked, flicking her hair over one shoulder.

Ethan shrugged. "She was looking at the photo gallery in the dining room this morning. I think she felt a little lost and out of place, so she just struck up a conversation with me, asking if I knew the people in the photos. You know, the people her age."

"Sort of like how she's striking up a conversation with Marcus now?" Charlotte suggested, her voice dripping with sarcasm. "Because she feels *so* lost and out of place?"

Brooke gazed at Valerie and Marcus from behind the protective shield of her dark lenses. In Brooke's experience, there were only two reasons why a tall, blonde, beautiful girl would compliment the looks of a complete stranger:

A) She was genuinely nice or incredibly open-minded or B) She had a hidden agenda.

Well, that's fine, Brooke thought mischievously. *I'm glad she thinks I look like Snow White. Maybe I can finally play that pure, sweet image to my advantage. Cinderella versus Snow White, huh?*

Too bad I'll be the one kissing the Prince.

Chapter Two

Mixing Things Up

Charlotte was the first to jump in the pool.

Bad move. She immediately resurfaced and splashed around for a minute, her teeth chattering. *CO-O-O-LD!* After a few sputtering gasps, she brushed her red curls from her eyes and launched into her breaststroke, even though she hated that word. She thought about her breasts (or rather, the lack thereof) way too often.

Charlotte von Klaus had been the first to do lots of things. She'd been the first to make out with a boy (Caleb Ramsey, in sixth grade, in a game of Spin the Bottle that had gotten slightly out of hand); the first to sneak into the downstairs sauna at Silver Oaks (on a dare from Brooke); and the first to take a slug of very pricey Pinot Noir straight from the bottle (after her parents' divorce last year. Luckily, with some brute force, Georgia had managed to wrestle the bottle away from Charlotte and toss it in the recycling bin).

And she was the first of her friends to see a therapist. And still the only one.

The way Charlotte saw it, if you were the first to do something, then you carved out some quality alone time — even if you were in the company of your two best friends.

Or, even if you were in the company of a boy. After all, she hadn't been thinking about Caleb Ramsey when she'd made out with him. She'd been thinking about her math homework, and walking Stella McCartney — the von Klaus family's smelly (male) Labrador — and which *South Park* rerun would be on that night.

So as Charlotte plowed through the icy water, kicking her legs and paddling, she didn't think about swimming. She thought about Marcus Craft.

Out of the corner of her eye, she could see him. Due to the overabundance of chlorine, he appeared extra fuzzy and dreamlike, and he was still languorously draped over the side of his chair, chatting up the Hot New Girl, Valerie What's-Her-Face, who had somehow snuck in under the radar. How had none of them heard of her before today? Even Ethan Brennan knew about her. It was absurd.

Breathe, stroke, kick . . . Breathe, stroke, kick . . . Breathe, stroke, kick . . .

Actually, what was more absurd was that Charlotte had to practice swimming.

For reasons never made clear, Old Fairfield Country Day — otherwise known as the Tombs (Charlotte coined the moniker herself after a freakish school field trip to Washington DC, but that was a very long story) — required that their students pass a swimming test in order to graduate. This was now the summer before senior year, and Charlotte was in big trouble. Brooke and Georgia would have no problem. Brooke had been a pool girl since birth. And there wasn't a single sport Georgia couldn't master.

Give her a bow and arrow; she'd become an archery champ in days. Hence, all of Charlotte's friends would say good-bye to the Tombs and attend college, whereas Charlotte envisioned herself flunking out and spiraling downward in a self-destructive binge of steak sandwiches until she became a grotesque tabloid headline:

1,543-LB WOMAN IS NEW GUINNESS WORLD RECORD HOLDER
FOR FATTEST HUMAN. "CAN'T LEAVE BED!!!" SHE SAYS.

Breathe, stroke, kick . . . Breathe, stroke, kick . . . Breathe, stroke, kick . . .

Charlotte reached the shallow end and nearly bumped her head on the stone steps. *Ugh.* She was about as grace-ful as a squid. Was Marcus watching her? She hoped not. On the other hand, if she started to drown, then Marcus would have to dive in and rescue her. But on the third hand (was there a third hand?), that would violate The Second Unspoken Rule of Silver Oaks, which Charlotte had writ-ten herself:

Thou shalt Not Poach Thy Friend's Love Interest.

Brooke was clearly interested in Marcus. Though that didn't mean that Charlotte couldn't still check him out. Their parents surreptitiously checked out their friends' sig-nificant others all the time, after all. It was the adult thing to do.

"How's the water?" a boy's voice asked.

Charlotte shook out her soaking red hair and turned to see Caleb Ramsey standing poolside, frowning.

Good lord, did that boy need some sun. As always, at this time of year, his lanky body was even whiter than Brooke's, especially in contrast with his oversized dark blue swim trunks and his mop of black hair. And as always, at this time of year, he somehow still managed to be completely adorable.

"Freezing, man," Charlotte said. "It's like *March of the Penguins* in here."

"Seriously, C."

"I am being serious. The good part is, much like said penguins, I have lots of blubber to keep me warm." Charlotte leaned against the side of the pool and rested her chin on her dripping arms, smiling up at him. "Unlike you."

"Will you do me a favor?" Caleb asked, returning the smile. "If you ever fish for a compliment again by claiming to be fat, will you give me permission to chop you up and bury you on the golf course?"

Charlotte stood up straight and saluted, deliberately splashing water on Caleb's knees. "Permission granted."

"Hey!" He laughed and scooted away. "Damn. That *is* cold."

"Once you're in, it gets better. I'm gonna do one more lap. My shrink says exercise is good for me." She launched into the water again.

Charlotte hadn't been able to joke around about therapy at first. She hadn't even told Brooke and Georgia that she was even *seeing* a shrink until after her second session post-divorce last year. Not because she was worried they would think she was a loon (they already knew that), but mostly because she wondered if they'd be hurt. After all, who needed a shrink when you've shared everything with your two best friends since the age of diapers?

Surprisingly, Brooke had been the first to speak up. "I think this is exactly what you need to do, sweetie," she'd said, squeezing Charlotte's hand. (This from the girl whose tenth-grade yearbook quote was: *"Life is far too important a thing to talk seriously about."* — Oscar Wilde.) And Charlotte began to realize Brooke was right. The difference between best friends and therapists? Best friends could and should constantly surprise you. Therapists couldn't and shouldn't. Dr. Gilmore was no exception. He'd worn the exact same paisley bow tie to every single session, now going on number fifty-four.

Charlotte reached the shallow end again, allowing her feet to touch the pool floor. She rubbed the water from her hair and eyes. Caleb was staring at Valerie now, though pretending not to. And Brooke was pretending to read *W,* and pretending not to watch Valerie and Marcus as well. Georgia was hurrying into the cabana to change, obviously about to meet Ethan on the tennis courts.

Caleb crouched down beside Charlotte, sitting on the edge of the tile and sticking his feet into the water. He eased them down very slowly, up to his knees, and then cringed, as if it were torture.

"You really are a wimp," Charlotte teased.

"Well, not all of us can be lifeguards." His voice dropped to a whisper. "By the way, have you met . . . ?" He didn't bother to finish the question.

"Sort of. I said hello to him, anyway. I still have yet to say hi to *her*."

Caleb glanced up at the lifeguard chair, and then returned his gaze to the water. He kicked his feet absently. "She seems pretty cool."

"Really? Have you talked to her?"

"No. This is the first time I've seen her."

"Easy there, Caleb. You're drooling."

"That's because of *you*, Charlotte," he said, rolling his eyes. "You know, I still haven't gotten over that game of Spin the Bottle."

Charlotte laughed in spite of herself. "Funny. I was just thinking about that."

"You were?" He puffed out his skinny chest. "I had that effect on you, huh?"

"Don't flatter yourself, stallion. Actually I was thinking about how I was thinking about other things. When we made out, you were the *last* thing on my mind."

"Thanks," Caleb said flatly. "I appreciate it."

"I didn't mean it like that. I was just thinking . . . I don't know."

"Very articulate," he mused.

"Hey, go easy on me. I got a C-minus in English this year."

"It's not your fault. You had Mr. Lowry. The guy's a sadist."

"No kidding," she grumbled. Charlotte stretched out and kicked her feet to keep warm. "Anyway, enough about the Tombs. It's summer. No school talk."

"Agreed. May the Tombs rest in peace. So what's with Brooke? She seems bummed."

"I think it's because —" Charlotte bit her lip. She was about to say: *This new girl is stealing her thunder.* But that wasn't fair to Brooke; besides, Brooke may *not* have been bummed. She may have been deeply involved in an article in *W,* a brilliant piece about the "25 Best Ways to Satisfy Your Man!"

"Because of what?" Caleb prodded.

"Because Ethan said the three of us are like a street gang," Charlotte replied, mostly because it was the first thing that came to mind.

"You're a lousy liar, Charlotte von Klaus," Caleb said with a laugh.

"He did say that!" she insisted, trying not to smile. "What? You don't believe me? Ask him."

"No, I believe you. And I agree. I'd say you three are exactly like a street gang. Except, you know, that you're socialites from Connecticut who spend all your time at the country club. That's the only difference."

"Is that what you really think of us?" She stopped kicking and stood, rubbing her wet arms. She wasn't sure why, but Caleb's jab had struck a chord inside her.

"Actually, no, I think what everyone else here thinks of you," he said, withdrawing his feet from the water. He made air quotes. "'Brooke, Georgia, and Charlotte,'" he proclaimed in a deep voice. "'The Princess, the Jock, and the Clown.'"

"Oh, God," Charlotte murmured, aghast. "That's even worse! Who thinks that?"

"Nobody." Caleb splashed her playfully. "I'm kidding. If anything, *you're* the princess." He stuck his big toe back in the water and splashed her. "Look, I should run. I have to escape before my parents get here. Are you gonna be around later?"

Charlotte nodded absently. She shivered and stared at the sunlight sparkling off the tiny pool waves.

"Hey, are you all right?" Caleb asked. "I was just messing around."

"I know, I know." She pushed back into the water. "I'm just in a weird mood. I guess we all are. End of school and all. And in August we're getting officially inducted into Silver Oaks, and all that crap."

"Yeah, well, welcome to my world," Caleb said wryly. "The world of weird moods." He sighed and turned, disappearing into the pool cabana.

Charlotte watched him go. What was she so upset about, anyway? And why should she care what anybody said about her and her friends, or, least of all, about Caleb Ramsey?

Maybe because she was scared that this summer *was* going to be more of the same old, same old. More hanging out by the pool. More of the same old banter with the same old pool *boys*: Caleb, and Ethan, and Robby Miller — another Old Fairfield Country Day kid — arrogant and in training to be a frat boy. And Robby's fratty friends, Mike and Johnny and Billy, who were all pretty much inter-changeable.

So maybe it was time to mix things up a little. Maybe somebody just had to make the first move.

Charlotte leaped out of the pool and marched right over to Marcus and Valerie, dripping water on the flagstones.

"Hi, again!" she said. "You're Valerie, right? Great to meet you." She extended a wet hand. "I'm Charlotte von Klaus. C for short. Welcome to Silver Oaks."